TERRY PRATCHETT

AIDED AND ABETTED BY

THE DISCWORLD EMPORIUM

PRESENTS

Mrs Bradshaw's Handbook

Dedicated to the memory of
Mr Archibald Bradshaw and Mr Ned Simnel,
early departures at the beginning of this particular journey

Mrs Bradshaw's Handbook

An illustrated guide to the railway

Produced in association with

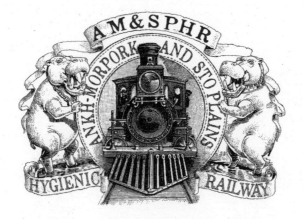

By Mrs Georgina Bradshaw

DOUBLEDAY

LONDON · NEW YORK · TORONTO · SYDNEY · AUCKLAND

MEMO:

To: *Harry King*

Please allow Mrs Georgina Bradshaw to travel anywhere she wants, even those little branch lines we haven't fully opened yet. She went to one of the best girls' schools I know of and understands language, and she is writing notes on all our destinations which may come in very useful. My instincts say that she will do us proud. I have an inkling that she will be either meticulous or humorous or, hopefully, both. And a widow who wears the kind of gold and diamond ring that she is wearing to travel through Ankh-Morpork and is still wearing it when she leaves is not going to be a fool. She speaks as well as Lady Sybil: that's Quirm College for you. Up School! Isn't this what we're after? We want people to widen their horizons on the train, of course, but why not day trips? You know what, there are people in Ankh-Morpork who haven't even got as far as Sto Lat yet. Travel broadens the mind, and also railway revenue.

Moist von Lipwig

MOIST VON LIPWIG
DIRECTOR AMSPHR

TRANSWORLD PUBLISHERS
61-63 Uxbridge Road, London W5 5SA
A Random House Group Company
www.transworldbooks.co.uk

First published in Great Britain
in 2014 by Doubleday
an imprint of Transworld Publishers

Additional illustrations by Peter Dennis
Text design by Lizzy Laczynska

A CIP catalogue record for this book
is available from the British Library.

ISBN 9780857522436

Addresses for Random House Group Ltd companies outside the UK
can be found at: www.randomhouse.co.uk
The Random House Group Ltd Reg. No. 954009

The Random House Group Limited supports the Forest Stewardship Council (FSC®), the
leading international forest-certification organization. Our books carrying the FSC label are
printed on FSC®-certified paper. FSC is the only forest-certification scheme endorsed by
the leading environmental organizations, including Greenpeace. Our paper procurement
policy can be found at www.randomhouse.co.uk/environment.

Printed and bound in Great Britain by
CPI Group (UK) Ltd, Croydon, CR0 4YY

2 4 6 8 10 9 7 5 3 1

CONTENTS

Dear Reader,

Since the demise of my darling husband Archibald, alas, I have had time on my hands, and so I set myself to travelling on the new railway. I have found the ambience of this mode of travel fascinating - it takes you where you want to go, and its continuing growth is wonderful. Who could dislike the railway? The naysayers told us that the railway would be almost the end of the world, foretelling that cows and sheep near the tracks would kill their young, and other dreadful occurrences. However, it would appear that out in the countryside the sight of a train actually enhances the landscape: watching a great train rounding a curve through woodland is a marvellous thing and it does something for the soul. It is well known that horses beside the railway will try to go faster than the train, with no ill effects, and the smoke passes quickly.

I have now journeyed hundreds of miles across the great Sto Plains and beyond - after all, one cannot mourn for ever. Wherever I go I gather what I trust will be useful information for the inexperienced traveller and this, together with my own observations, is the subject of this publication.

Many of our citizens already use the railway for business and commercial travel. My hope is that people may be encouraged to travel for both recreational and educational purposes. For this reason information is included on destinations which would interest the curious traveller as well as the family on holiday. It is certainly true that experiencing the sights and sounds of new lands and meeting new people has been an

adventure for me and one that I would like others to share. If I can make a fellow traveller's journey that bit more comfortable and rewarding then I will have achieved what I set out to do.

You will also find here information about places of accommodation and refreshment that I have visited, annotated with my personal comments. I hope these will prove helpful, but they are by no means exhaustive, and should travellers wish to update this publication in the light of their own experience they should write to Messrs Goatberger, Brewer Street, Isle of Gods, Ankh-Morpork, the publishers of this volume.

The directors of the AM&SPHR have afforded me every assistance in my quest and I am pleased to say have even acted on many of my suggestions to improve the well-being and safety of the passenger.

I look forward to meeting more of those who, like me, are fascinated with this wonder of our age, not least those young men now known humorously as 'train spotters', who amaze me with their knowledge of everything about the railway. They are its soul writ large in their little books, and I admire their useful attire. Indeed, I had my dressmaker make me something similar, so I am now an Anorankh myself.

To all my friends: Good Bashing!*

Georgina Bradshaw

---

* The uninitiated may wish to note that bashing is much like spotting, the difference being that bashing involves actually riding on trains.

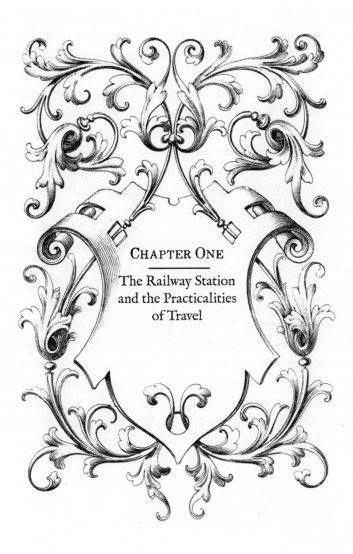

CHAPTER ONE

The Railway Station
and the Practicalities
of Travel

I
___

The recently completed New Ankh Station, Ankh-Morpork, is now the city's principal railway terminus, the point of departure for all trains to the Sto Plains and to Quirm, so it is here that we begin our journey. It is a fine building with a grand façade and a large open entrance hall where a greenish light filters through the great stained-glass windows of the front elevation. Inside is a bustling cacophony of sounds and sights: the blast of the magnificent engines as they discharge great bursts of steam, the whistles of guards, slamming of doors, people shouting, and sometimes livestock bellowing as it is brought to market from the Sto Plains. And then there is the hubbub of itinerant sellers of beverages, food, newspapers and nostrums, and the blare of the loud-hailers announcing train arrivals and departures.

For the inexperienced traveller this can be a confusing and alarming experience. My advice is to make your way straight to the booking office by the main station entrance; it is clearly signposted. Here you may obtain your ticket and seat reservation as well as information on train departures, fares, platforms and journey times.

NOTICE

The Ankh-Morpork and Sto Plains Hygienic Railway is pleased to offer the following standard travel arrangements. To enquire about group rates or private hire please contact the station master. Individuals with special requirements outside the scope of our standard provision should write to Mr Moist von Lipwig.

FIRST CLASS

The first class passenger is offered every comfort and the purchase of a seat in this class includes space in the luggage van for the accommodation of trunks and servants. Private windowless carriages with secure tiered biers for the safe transportation of caskets are available on the Altiplano Express.

Our first class dining carriage offers cuisine from all over the Disc cooked by the finest chefs. Produce is always fresh and those passengers who enjoy the hunt are welcome to test their skills from a moving train and have their game prepared en route. Condiments are included.

Passengers may dine from their own hampers should religious or dietary requirements make this necessary, as might be the case for, say, Nugganites, or Black Ribbon vampires (rare steak available).

Our first class travellers have exclusive use of a luxury convenience (separate facilities for ladies include luxury soap and fresh flowers). A mahogany step and reduced-aperture seat is available, on request, for dwarf travellers.

SECOND CLASS

Designed for those who choose to practise a prudent economy, without undue sacrifice of comfort, this service we offer is second to one.

Seats are sprung and there are luggage racks for hand-held baggage with secure van space available at a modest cost for trunks. A dining car is provided offering wholesome foods at a variety of prices.

For the convenience of passengers in this class a washroom cubicle can be found in each carriage.

THIRD CLASS

Suitable for the honest worker or servants of the better sort. The carriage is completely weatherproof and fixed wooden benches are provided with space beneath for the storage of small items of luggage. A trolley service offers refreshment on long-distance trains.

At the discretion of the guard, troll passengers may be asked to move to different accommodation for weight considerations. Reinforced open carriages are provided for those of a larger persuasion (premium rate for travel at the front of the train). We are pleased to announce that our special two-tier carriages are now available for dwarfs, gnomes, goblins and others for whom low ceilings are no hindrance, who wish to take advantage of a special cut-price tariff.

Note: Unaccompanied children are not eligible for this tariff, regardless of species.

Unlike coach travel (whether by mail or stage), where one has to contend with exposure to the weather, a railway journey now offers enclosed seating for all classes, and sheltered platforms at which to entrain and alight.

In addition it is possible for the single lady to travel in a 'Ladies Only' carriage if she wishes, though I find that more diverting conversation may often be had in a mixed carriage. There are various classes of travel to suit all pockets and needs. Not everyone can afford the luxury of first class; the new second class tariff is quite satisfactory for most people.

If you are undertaking several journeys or planning to travel on a regular basis it is well worth investing in what Mister Lipwig has called a 'Mollusc Card'. With one of these in your purse, the world will indeed become your Mollusc as this card entitles the bearer to travel far and wide for a single subscription.

Passengers with heavy luggage may like to use the services of a station porter (often a troll), who will collect the trunks from your coach or cart and deposit them on the train. (Be aware that trolley buses are not allowed to come as far as the platforms; save yourself the embarrassment of a refusal.) Make sure that any luggage travelling in the van is clearly labelled with your name and destination. This is especially important if you plan to travel as far as Uberwald and beyond where unlabelled trunks are often subject to inspection. It is general practice to give your porter a small gratuity thus providing him with a tax-free addition to his meagre wage. In expectation of this he will not drop your luggage and will assist you to the correct train and carriage. With any luck he will remember you on your return. (He will certainly remember you if your tip fails to come up to his expectations, and, being a modern, get-ahead Ankh-Morpork troll, will have read your labels.)

As well as the itinerant pedlars of goods there are tea-shops, cafés and bars providing refreshment of all kinds on the station concourse, together with bookshops, haberdashers (though one wonders why any sensible person

would leave the purchase of a pair of socks until they are catching a train), stationers and tobacconists.

Separate waiting rooms are provided for single ladies, or gentlemen and families. Public conveniences for ladies, gentlemen and dwarfs are well signposted.

Should you have the misfortune to mislay any item, there is a Lost Property Office run under the auspices of the Guild of Thieves.

LOST PROPERTY
& LEFT LUGGAGE

The Ankh-Morpork Thieves' Guild operates (under an exclusive licence) the LOST PROPERTY AND LEFT LUGGAGE OFFICES at all major terminals.

THE LOST PROPERTY OFFICE is open Monday to Sunday from ten in the morning until midnight and from noon until five in the afternoon on Octeday.

Items not collected within a week may be repurchased at the Sunday cart-tail sale held in Pleaders Row at the back of the Guild Building.

Any weapons found will be handed in to the City Watch; body parts will be given to their resident Igor for proper care (except for wooden legs, dentures and glass eyes, which will be held in the main office). Livestock will be held in the dog pound.

Lost children will be held in the crèche on platform 1 under the watchful eye of Mrs Chokeum.

Please NOTE: a fee (on a sliding scale) is required in all transactions.

LEFT LUGGAGE OFFICES

These are available at all main-line stations and offer the traveller the opportunity, for a fee, to leave luggage and other possessions in a safe place for up to two days.

Please NOTE: Left Luggage is NOT cheap accommodation, nor is it a repository for infirm or dead relatives, a mail address, a retail or fast food preparation area, a venue for impromptu stage performances or a place to send the confused or terminally vague.

THE THIEVES' GUILD TRAVELLER'S GUARANTEE

This is an enhanced service available from the Thieves' Guild that can be included in your rail ticket at extra cost, ensuring no loss on your journey from any LICENSED THIEF. This gives the traveller peace of mind and the assurance that the Thieves' Guild, operating as it does a Zero Tolerance Policy on any unlicensed thievery, will guarantee a secure journey for the passenger and their possessions.

USUAL TERMS & CONDITIONS APPLY.

The Thieves' Guild of Ankh-Morpork extends its influence throughout the Ankh-Morpork Hegemony. Mostly.
Outside this area, any theft or loss is a matter for the local Watch or such agencies as exist.

The station boasts a public clacks office and an accurate clock. Members of the goblin community who, I have been told, have a great affinity with all things mechanical, ensure the smooth running of both of these modern devices. Such is the clock's prominence it has become a recognized place to meet fellow travellers.

We know that the railway has opened new possibilities for commerce and leisure but there is another body of men who have seen an opportunity to take their mission for saving souls further afield and at a greater pace than ever before. Hence the prominent sign indicating the 'Assembly Point for the Church of Om Mission' on the concourse. Young missionaries, their bright clean faces just visible under broad-brimmed hats like black soup dishes, trudge joyfully off, their hearts filled with religious zeal and on their lips one of their church's interminable tuneless hymns. Like black snails they bear massive backpacks hung with cooking pots, spare sandals and the like, and filled with religious tracts; some are even pulling small

harmoniums as they make their way to the train heading hubwards towards dark forests and the dangers that lurk within.

Devotees of that new pursuit 'train spotting' are easily recognized by their all-weather dress and look of somebody trying to see everything at once, especially should 'everything' include a new train. I must caution my friends the spotters to take care at all times – some of the light trains travel quietly. For members of the spotting fraternity who would like to get behind the scenes of the railway, tours are available upon application to the station master. I have noticed that these are often very full, since it appears that practically everybody in the world is now a train spotter.

In the short time I have been travelling I have witnessed a plethora of contraptions aiming to capture the waiting passenger's dollar spring up on station platforms. They purport to tell you your weight or stamp you out a small metal label with your name on, or even take your iconograph portrait. Enterprises of this kind have greatly increased the numbers of imps in employment, and concerns have been raised in some quarters about their working conditions, including allegations of illegal imp-trafficking organized by gangs with connections to the Breccia. Some machines dispense a somewhat stale-looking

confection; however, beware: often you may hear a coin - whether your own or another hopeful traveller's - clank into the machine's receptacle but nothing emerges despite all manner of hammering. Perhaps the Thieves' Guild should conduct an investigation into the status of these devices.

Once you are on the departure platform you will hear final announcements made by loud-hailer. The instructions are sometimes a little difficult to understand as the natural enthusiasm of the announcers, many of them members of the Guild of Town Criers obliged to change their employment since the advent of the newspapers, encourages them to try to out-shout each other. Further confusion is caused when information is being transmitted in both Morporkian and Dwarfish as is sometimes the case.

NOTICE

When the train's departure is announced any person in the carriage not intending to travel must leave the train immediately.

●●●●●●●●●●●●

The AM&SPHR takes no responsibility for persons who ignore this warning and find themselves being transported contrary to their intentions. A full fare will be charged including the cost of the return journey.

●●●●●●●●●●●●

The deliberate abandoning of elderly relatives or children on a train without a valid ticket is an offence under Railway Act number 3387/b.

●●●●●●●●●●●●

The AM&SPHR takes no responsibility for persons who by reason of deafness or other disability do not hear the aforementioned announcement.

●●●●●●●●●●●●

The AM&SPHR takes no responsibility for dwarfs whose protective headgear prevents them from hearing the aforementioned announcement.

PREPARING FOR YOUR JOURNEY

When you undertake any but the shortest railway journey there is a great deal to be thought about and arrangements to be made before you set out from home for the station.

DOCUMENTS AND CURRENCY

This new Railway Age of swift, comfortable, affordable transport has seen a great increase in the number of people travelling to foreign parts. Ankh-Morpork families who, only a year or two ago, would have looked on a journey to Sto Lat as a once-in-a-decade - or even once-in-a-lifetime - experience, now take day trips to Quirmian beaches, and plan rambling holidays in the Ramtops. Border guards across the continent have been overwhelmed by the unprecedented numbers of international visitors, and as a result are now far more likely to demand a valid passport to stamp, as opposed to whatever bit of paper the traveller might have upon their person.

Before embarking on your journey check carefully what documents are required by the states lying on your chosen route.

While a passport is not always essential for travel to Quirm it is useful to have by you for identification. People seeking to relocate, retire or buy derelict farmhouses to renovate in Quirm should visit the Quirmian Embassy in Park Lane to complete an application form for a resident's visa.

The Ankh-Morpork Foreign Affairs Office will issue a visitor's visa for entry into Uberwald. Dwarfs visiting the 'Homeland' for the first time will need a valid birth certificate from their local or family grag which will enable them to get a travel permit from the Legation of the Low King. Historically there have been few restrictions on troll movements (at least outside the city of Bonk), but due to a recent increase in the smuggling of illegal substances a valid travel permit, obtainable from the Embassy of the Diamond King of Trolls, is now a requirement.

Foreign currency may be obtained from the Royal Bank of Ankh-

Morpork and the Royal Overseas Bank. The AM dollar is acceptable in Quirm, and, as you would expect, gold is welcome everywhere regardless of whose head appears on it; but travellers to Uberwald will need to take some bizots for smaller transactions.

A reputable travel agent may be commissioned to obtain all necessary documentation and currency for your journey in addition to booking your rail tickets and making hotel reservations. However, this 'bundle' service may not suit the independent-minded traveller; moreover there have been reports of bogus agents, whose financial standing and know-how is, to say the least, dubious, leaving people abandoned in half-built hotels and with no return ticket.

ARTICLES TO INCLUDE IN YOUR HAND LUGGAGE

Even though the rail passenger is well protected from the elements it can be cold in winter and it is only sensible to wear warm clothing and take a small rug for added protection. On some far hubward lines a Lancre wool travel blanket is provided by the railway company.

I have found the following items can add to the enjoyment of the journey.

☞ A potpourri of fresh lavender or cologne according to preference; on some rural branch lines you may well find you are sharing your carriage with a farmer taking his goat or pig to market. It is as well to be prepared.

☞ A modest bag of peppermints - always refreshing - and a small flask of brandy for emergencies.

☞ A vial of eyewash in case of smuts to the eye. (If possible sit with your back to the engine.) A small bottle of solvent is also useful, to remove soot and stains from gloves.

☞ A book to read or crossword to employ the mind will pass the time if you travel alone and a small notebook and pencil is indispensable for recording useful facts.

☞ A long journey can become quite a convivial occasion, with fellow

travellers sharing their stories and experiences. In such congenial circumstances, having a game to hand can add to the enjoyment of all present: consider including in your bag a pack of cards, or one of the admirably compact chess sets now available. 'Travellers' Thud', however, is still too large an item for any but the most committed player to transport.

Refreshments on the Train

Long-distance trains include a restaurant car where the traveller can have a hot meal, though this amenity may be restricted to holders of a first class ticket. A buffet carriage will offer beverages and snacks to all, and for passengers travelling in third class or on local trains there will usually be a trolley service. Thankfully the strict regulations of the railway company allow no such gastronomic horror as the un-named meat pie or sausage-in-a-bun offered on the city streets by unlicensed vendors.

The passenger of limited means may prefer to take advantage of the easily transportable comestibles which may be purchased from approved vendors on the station. Chief among these is a version of the Miner's Pasty, in origin a sort of pie that could survive a forty-foot drop on to a hard rock. Now adapted by the accomplished chef Mr All Jolson for consumption on our railways, this pasty is a substantial meal, containing at one end a named meat and two veg, in the middle a serviette and fork, and at the other end rhubarb and custard. Less extravagant versions are popular with the footplate crew who heat them on a shovel over the fire-box; they remain edible without the use of a chisel, mostly.

In my journeys I have often witnessed the kindness of travellers who are willing to share their food with a complete stranger. If you do plan to take a picnic it is now the custom to pack extra provisions to distribute to your immediate neighbours in the carriage. It always breaks the ice. On a recent journey to Big Cabbage I was seated next to an elderly gentleman who unpacked from his case several bottles of different patent medicines for digestive disorders. Having dosed himself he tucked a brightly coloured napkin into his collar and proceeded to balance on his knee a fine china tureen in which were assembled a brace of pig's trotters, half a dozen pickled eggs, pickled onions, pickled plums, a small mountain of pickled red cabbage, a selection of chutneys and several types of mustard. The gentleman who offered this vinegary selection to his neighbours revealed that his lady wife ran her own pickling business and he was a martyr to her stock control system. It seems that any preserve approaching the end of its

"Premium People Pick a Premium Pickle"

Available at all good stockists and over the counter at your local pharmacy

edible life was put in his packed lunch that he might share it among fellow travellers and thus introduce potential customers to the delights of Mrs Staines's Tracklements.

Another interesting meal I encountered was the one I shared with a dwarf who was travelling from Zemphis to Ohulan Cutash. It was kind of him to offer and it would have been churlish of me to refuse his generosity. He produced a small brown paper bag filled with rat pâté sandwiches made using traditional dwarf bread. The dry curling crusts were as hard as iron and just as inedible and the pâté could have done the duty of shoe leather. Even now whenever I come across a badly prepared or indigestible sandwich I compare it in my mind to the railway sandwich I encountered just outside Zemphis.

EXCURSIONS WITHOUT ALARMS

Ladies, there is a lot of nonsense whispered in drawing rooms about the supposed dangers facing the female traveller on our railway. I mention

them only so that I can allay your concerns with my own observations.

Some silly girls say that the speed of the train is such that should you put your head outside the carriage window when the train is in motion it will be torn off by the force of the blast of passing air. Well, you may lose your hat if it is not securely pinned, and you may possibly get a smut in your eye, but that is probably the worst that can occur, unless of course you are unlucky enough to meet a train going in the opposite direction.

Maiden aunts may say that the rhythmic vibration of the train over the tracks causes upset to the female anatomy such as palpitations and flushes. Indeed they add, I suspect more in hope than fear, the assertion that this same vibration inflames the male traveller, leading to unwanted advances to any woman in the vicinity. I met one poor young woman who had been frightened by her grandmother into holding a pin between her lips when going through tunnels in case someone tried to kiss her. Personally I find the motion of the train not the least bit unpleasant and if anything it has a gently soporific effect.

The suggestion that you need to take a remedy prior to travelling on the train to combat motion sickness is, I am afraid, an invention put about by the manufacturers of such nostrums and made purely for their commercial gain.

None the less the railway is a new form of travel and certain safety restrictions apply which passengers need to conform to for their own well-being and that of fellow travellers. I attach an up-to-date notice for your information.

NOTICE

1. Travelling on the roof of the train is prohibited. The only exception made is for Harpies, in view of their usefulness as audible warnings at level crossings.

2. To open the door of the carriage before the train has stopped moving may cause serious injury to both passers-by and passengers. Bogeymen must not remove carriage doors or replace existing doors with their own.

3. To leave the train while it is in motion is forbidden. The track may well pass by your door, but alighting from the train between stations is a serious hazard and can cause delays for other passengers when deep-cleaning staff have to be called to the scene as a result.

4. Passengers are reminded that the lighting of fires (open or closed) in the carriage is not permitted.

5. For the comfort of fellow passengers please refrain from singing or playing any musical instrument (especially the accordion) while on the train. The Patrician's office has

also advised that under the Acts prohibiting street theatre, the railway is to be defined as a street.

6 Walking, picnicking, camping and the playing of ball-games on the track is strictly prohibited as is the placing thereon of any obstruction such as barbecues, goal posts, or sales kiosks.

7 The use of tunnels for mushroom farming, conversion to domestic dwelling (except by authorized troll employees), or industrial premises is strictly forbidden.

8 Mining, excavations and prospecting are not to be undertaken in or via any tunnel, embankment, viaduct or track. It will be held to be a felony under the Railways Act and the statutes of the Low King.

NOTE: All tracks, sleepers, machinery (static and moving) and all other property belonging to or under the hire of the Ankh-Morpork & Sto Plains Hygienic Railway is protected by Thieves' Guild Policy No 30054b. Any unlicensed theft will be dealt with terminally by the Thieves' Guild.

LIVESTOCK (Domestic)
Accompanied dogs are permitted in the carriage, but other domestic animals must be crated for travel in the van. This includes swamp dragons, which are only allowed on the train if they have an up-to-date certificate of good health and are not fed on the journey.

REFRESHMENTS AT THE STATION

MRS BUNCE'S CAFÉ
Offers wholesome and fresh food, much of which comes from her capacious frying pan.

. . . .

WINKLE'S BAR
Run by the celebrated Ankh-Morpork brewery, offers fresh oysters in season, fine dark ales and porters. The pork pies and other finger foods are robust in flavour and generous in portion. Standing room only.

. . . .

JOLSON'S RESTAURANT
A fine array of local Ankh-Morpork dishes cooked to perfection. Allow enough time to fully enjoy and digest these generous meals before starting your journey. Slumpie is a speciality.

. . . .

GIMLET'S RAT-TO-GO KIOSK
A favourite among our dwarf community with a reputation well deserved for the quality of produce. The 'Rat Wrap to Go' has been designed with the traveller in mind: there is no leakage of ketchup or ratty juices. Guaranteed no beef.

. . . .

PUSHPRAM WINKLE STALL
A pint of fresh winkles is a most nourishing and economical meal best eaten on the platform before you travel. Pins supplied.

THE PASTY MASTER

Get YOURSELF a PASTY On Board!

ALL JOLSON

All Jolson
All Flavour
All Fresh

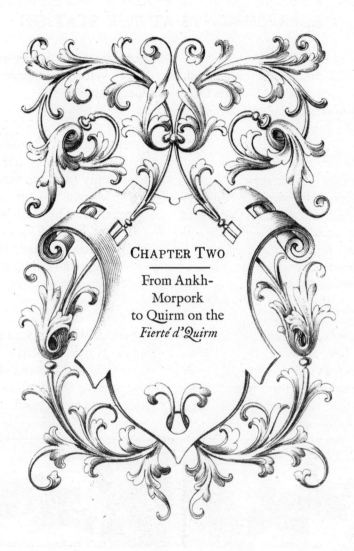

CHAPTER TWO

From Ankh-
Morpork
to Quirm on the
Fierté d'Quirm

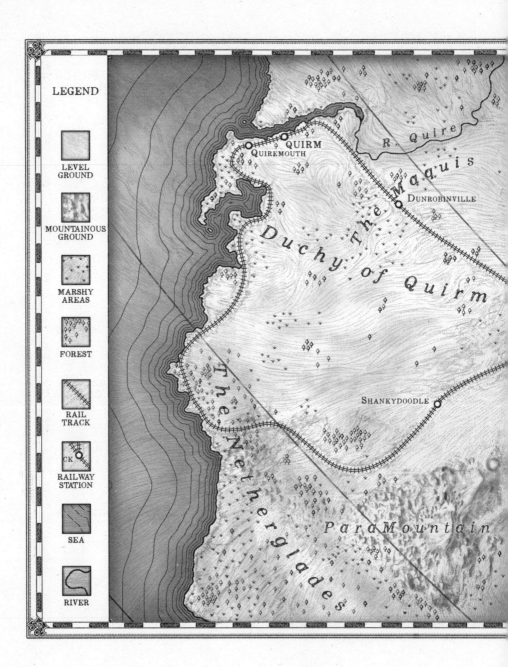

LEGEND

LEVEL
GROUND

MOUNTAINOUS
GROUND

MARSHY
AREAS

FOREST

RAIL
TRACK

CK

RAILWAY
STATION

SEA

RIVER

QUIRM
QUIREMOUTH

R. Quire

The Maquis

DUNROBINVILLE

Duchy of Quirm

The Netherglades

SHANKYDOODLE

ParaMountain

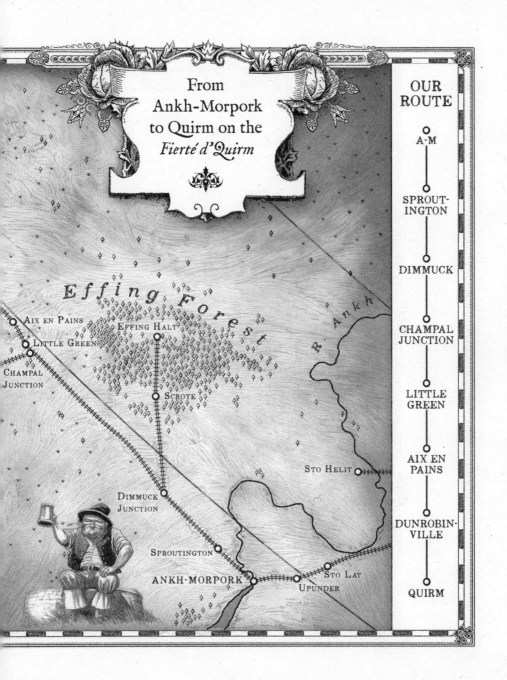

From
Ankh-Morpork
to Quirm on the
Fierté d'Quirm

OUR
ROUTE

A-M

SPROUT-
INGTON

DIMMUCK

CHAMPAL
JUNCTION

LITTLE
GREEN

AIX EN
PAINS

DUNROBIN-
VILLE

QUIRM

AIX EN PAINS

LITTLE GREEN

CHAMPAL
JUNCTION

Effing Forest

EFFING HALT

SCROTE

R. Ankh

STO HELIT

DIMMUCK
JUNCTION

SPROUTINGTON

ANKH-MORPORK

UPUNDER

STO LAT

2

The *Fierté d'Quirm* Express leaves New Ankh Station from platform 3 at ten in the morning. The first class carriages on this train are commodious, having upholstered seats with ample space for a handbag and, above the seat, a most useful shelf to stow an overnight case. I believe it is the good taste of Lady King that is responsible for the attractive curtains at the windows. These match the design of the seat velour which features a repeating pattern of cabbages.

As the train leaves the station it has to negotiate a complicated mesh of criss-crossing tracks where locomotives pass each other and clattering goods wagons are noisily shunted. These movements are all controlled by the signalmen from their strategically placed elevated sheds.

A few minutes out of the station the train approaches the recently completed New Ankh Bridge, a wonder of modern engineering and design. A troll wearing a bright yellow waistcoat uses his megaphone to alert any workers on the bridge to keep clear and then gravely raises his arm to indicate that the train may continue. There is a fine view up-river

to the old Water Gate and ships at anchor in the docks. The sooty plumes of smoke rising from the forest of chimneys occlude any view of the finer architectural features of the city, but the top of that famous landmark the Tower of Art can be seen and on a clear day the great clacks tower on the Tump is visible.

The train speeds up as it clears the last vestiges of the city and suddenly we are in open countryside. Refreshments are offered by a smartly dressed

steward and the fresh coffee presented in a fine china cup is most welcome. The railway makes travelling so much more comfortable and I am sure that soon the long, slow coach journeys along pot-holed roads at the mercy of bad weather and indifferent suspension will be a thing of the past.

From the window of the train one can see well-constructed farmsteads surrounded by neat fields of potatoes and beans as well as the ever present cabbages. After about half an hour's travel the train slows on the approach to the small town of Sproutington.

•SPROUTINGTON•

POPULATION: 446
CLACKS TERMINAL: *at the station.*
POST OFFICE: *in the town square.*
MARKET DAY: *Saturday.*
Bean Fair third Tuesday in Sektober.
Sproutington is the centre of the bean drying and packaging industry. Sproutington Hall, once the country seat of the Snapcases, is now occupied by the Bendigo family.

Here the track runs along an embankment which allows a good view of Sproutington Hall, its grand ivy-covered façade and barley-sugar chimneys now almost eclipsed by the giant advertising boards proclaiming the virtues of Bendigo's Beans. One sincerely hopes that the late Lord Snapcase is turning in his grave, allowing a small comfort to those who suffered under his governance.

After the main bean harvest

in Sektober, the locals make a special pottage of the gleanings. This 'Bean Feast' or 'Flatulent Tuesday' sometimes coincides with the Soul Cake Duck celebrations. A fellow traveller advised me to avoid the town during this period. It seems that the seasonal peak in excess digestive gases, combined with home-distilled bean liquor, makes for an explosive occasion which can lead to sometimes fatal accidents.

Over the next half-hour the view from the train hardly changes but the land rises gradually to the second stop on the route, Dimmuck Junction.

Here one can transfer to the branch line running up to Scrote and Effing Halt.

•DIMMUCK•

POPULATION: 656
CLACKS TERMINAL: *in the station.*
POST OFFICE
ACCOMMODATION: *Station Hotel, Cooper's Arms.*
BANK: *Ankh-Morpork Mercantile, open Wednesday and Friday.*
MARKET DAY: *Wednesday.*
Earth-up Friday Fair in June, the Chitting Fair mid-Ick.
Since the development of the branch line to the Effing Forest, Dimmuck has become the centre of a busy joinery industry.

Even from the train the traveller is assailed by the smell of sawn timber and wood preservative and the sound of sawing, sanding and hammering. Since the opening of the Effing Forest line which brings the renowned and colourful Effing timber to Ankh-Morpork there have developed myriad workshops making furniture and small decorative items such as trinket boxes.

The old stone shrine to Epidity is now much neglected, which is a pity as these monuments are becoming increasingly rare. In the days when potatoes were the main source of income and a sack of

Dimmuck's prize mashers fetched a fair price at market, the good people of the town decorated the shrine once a year on 'Earth-up Friday' with garlands of flowers and potato croquettes. A potato queen was crowned and children had a day off school to help in the fields.

I recall passing by Dimmuck many years ago when it was a hamlet of just a few small dilapidated farms. The people looked malnourished and the children had no shoes. Now they look prosperous and well dressed and even if there are perhaps too many establishments selling potato gin and sawdust scrumpy, it is part of the price we pay for this economic growth fuelled by the railway.

After Dimmuck the train travels through a landscape of mixed farming, where fields of cows and pigs break up the monotony of arable crops; and looking hubwards it is possible to see the fringes of the Effing Forest. It is an hour and a half to Champal Junction where the slow train branches off towards

the coast. During this journey the view changes and gentle hills and valleys replace the plains. If you are travelling in May you will witness a most enchanting sight: acres of apple orchards in full blossom, a sweet-smelling pink and white lace covering everything as far as the eye can see, and looking rimwards this lovely view is topped off by the snowy summit of Para Mountain.

The track passes a curious monument called Putter's Result. It is a column with what appears to be an apple on the top; I had seen it from the road many years ago and learnt its history but never had an opportunity to examine the splendid workmanship. The story goes that sometime in our long history there was a revolt by the peasants in the area who were suffering from the usual depredations of poor harvests and exorbitant rents. There was a bit of rick-burning, a few pitchforks were raised and there were scuffles in the local hostelry. The arrival on the scene of Lord Selachii's Light Infantry to 'put down the oiks' polarized local opinion to such an extent that half a dozen

angry farmers led by a night-soil man called Horatio Chumbunderly became an armed band ready to do battle. At this stage accounts of

the debacle vary, but it appears that both forces unaccountably discovered a cache of cider in their midst. The inevitable inebriation was compounded by the cider's medicinal nature and the two armies became one body of men sharing a common affliction and in search of a privy. The outcome was that concessions were made by both sides and no blood was shed. The relieved local population raised a subscription to have the monument erected, on the site of the privy, to commemorate Putter's Russett, the local cider apple.

The train stops for some time on the approach to the station at Champal Junction with the apologies of the guard. It seems that when the branch line from this station was being constructed, track laying began from the coast instead of from Champal. As the work neared completion it became apparent that all was not going to plan and the new line, instead of joining at Champal Town station, missed it by a few hundred yards. The surveyors blamed local residents, who were against the railway, for interfering with the gauging rods; the locals blamed goblins. Whatever the cause, the end result is that trains to the coast have to be shunted backwards out of the station after making their stop, to join the branch line. It certainly causes some confusion for passengers joining the train here as it is not always easy to establish the destination of the train as it goes back and forth past the platforms.

•CHAMPAL TOWN•

POPULATION: 765
CLACKS TERMINAL: *at the station.*
POST OFFICE: *Castle Square.*
ACCOMMODATION: *Castle Hotel, The Selachii Arms.*

MARKET DAY: *Wednesday.*
Mid-May Apple Queen Parade,
Sektober cider festival.
A pleasant market town in the midst of orchards and fruit farms which provide the main income for the population.
The old castle overlooking the town was

:

once part of King Lorenzo the Kind's defences. The keep is well preserved but the curtain walls are sadly depleted, much of the stone having been used to build dwellings, apple stores and barns to house cider presses.

From Champal Junction station travellers can take a coach to the centre of the town which is certainly worth a visit. There are splendid views from the old castle keep, which houses a fine collection of man traps, woman snares and children's gins, and other implements of torture personally designed by Lorenzo the Kind. (The iron maiden which normally would be part of this collection has been removed and in a modified form serves as a most efficient apple crusher.)

A culinary speciality of Champal is ice cream, made by the Glissops, a local farming family. They have taken over the large ice-houses which were previously used to store fish in the days when it was brought by road to Ankh-Morpork. It is said by some people that a slightly fishy aroma still prevails, giving an unusual piquancy to this icy confection.

The current border with Quirm lies just five miles from Champal, in a village called Little Green by the Morporkian residents and

Petty Chou by the Quirmians.

It is marked by a dilapidated five-bar gate across the track with peeling white paint. The train stops here for ten minutes, supposedly to give the border guard an opportunity to inspect travellers' documentation. It certainly gives the owner of Fat Sally's, a local café, a chance to offer a 'fried slice' to everyone on the train and, I notice, supply a very large plateful of fried comestibles to the engine crew.

I share with my readers an extract from a report held in the archive of the Guild of Trespassers, describing this border crossing as it was a hundred years ago, at the start of the Century of the Fruitbat. Not much seems to have changed.

FAT SALLY'S
Plat Du Jour
—— •◦• ——
Where Quirmian cuisine
meets
Ankh-Morpork's appetite
—— •◦• ——

FRIED PÂTÊ &
GRAVEY 3P

SOSS, EGG, FRIED
SLICE AND FROGS
LEGGES 20P

WALL FRUIT 2P

CHEESE
3P

PROPER CHEESE
6P

ALL SERVED WITH AVEC

To Major S. Pillitt (retired), Explorers' Society
25th Grune, Little Green Border Post.

Dear Sir,

As directed I rode to the customs post that marks the border between the
state of Ankh-Morpork and the Duchy of Quirm. There is a border here in
the same way you get a tidemark on the strand: not exactly visible, more an
indication of ebb and flow. I have seen more significant boundaries between
village foot-the-ball teams. There is a shack with an open side and a tall
rusty chimney which reeks with the smell of ancient bacon. The person
running the establishment was, by the look of her, her own best customer.
Quirm was represented by a small garden shed in which, lurking like over-
large skittles, were two of the fattest men I had ever seen. They were wearing
ill-fitting faded blue uniforms topped with a small peaked cap that rose on
each head like a pill box. I proffered my papers and they were taken up and,
without scrutiny, placed on a rickety table that was littered with bottles of
wine and overflowing ashtrays. One of the guards produced a rubber stamp
from his pocket which he pressed into an ink-soaked rag and used to endorse
the passport. This formality done I was waved through into what appeared
to be someone's back garden. I believe that your proposed expedition to Quirm
will not meet with any difficulties via this route.

Yours faithfully,

Jeremy Plight. MES

Ten miles on, the grand chateau of Aix en Pains comes into view, surrounded by acres of vineyard.

The vineyard welcomes visitors and offers wine-tasting as well as a guided tour of the winery and the chateau gardens. The best time of year to visit is Sektober, when the rare Better-late-than-never Lilies are in bloom - and fortuitously this coincides with the grape harvest. Two grape varieties (Risibling and Muscrat) are grown on the chalky Rim-facing slopes and from these a very acceptable full-bodied red and a fruity white wine are produced. Traditional methods are used to extract the grape juice and the sight of a bunch of jolly workers, knee-deep in a vat of purple juice, trousers rolled to the thigh and singing as they pummel the crop with their feet, would make anyone smile.

There is a small dining room at the winery where guests can sample local dishes with a glass or two of the latest vintage. A clever fusion of cooking styles combines the sophistication of Quirmian 'Avec-cuisine' with the filling and substantial Ankh-Morpork diet. Thus on the day I visited the 'plate of the day' was Clooty Soufflé avec pickled green cabbage and a purée of lickun berries.

Leaving the pleasant surroundings of the chateau, the land rises to an arid plain and subsistence-level farms give way to scrubland. The train picks up speed and the only signs of civilization visible amid the dense thickets of black thorn are the ochre mine workings, scoured by a hot wind that is as dry as burnt toast and just as gritty. The train races through Dunrobinville station without stopping; apparently it is a request stop and used exclusively by the landowner, who is reputed to be a retired bandit. Two and a half hours after leaving the Quirmian border the train runs downhill, through the shadow of a deep cutting, until the view opens up revealing the walled city of Quirm basking in sunshine. The railway runs parallel to the River Quire, and between the trees lining its banks it is usually possible to glimpse one of the

famous Quire river boats.

As a girl I travelled on one of these great river boats; their opulence is equalled by the olfactory assault from the huge oxen that power them and the river can be treacherous. Yet another good reason to travel by rail.

•QUIRM•

POPULATION: 13,054

CLACKS TERMINALS: *railway station, City Watch HQ, Grand Hotel and main post office.*

POST OFFICE: *Place de Malle.*

ACCOMMODATION: *The Duchy Hotel, The Grand Hotel, The New Pavilion.*

BANKS: *Quirm Banking Company, Quire Associates.*

THE CITY WATCH: *located in the Rue-de-Wakening.*

DAILY FISH MARKET: *at Porte Odeur.*

GENERAL MARKETS: *Wednesday and Saturday.*

A Floral Parade takes place on the last weekend in May. The Scallop Fair is celebrated in Spune.

Quirm Castle, a good example of dynastic architecture, is located on a small prominence by the City Wall. It is home to Lord Rodley, Duke of Quirm; his mother, Brenda, now resides in the nearby Dower House.

The main commercial activities of the area are fishing, viticulture, cheese-making and rare toffee mining. The new toffee refinery built by the Worthe family is scarcely visible behind a screen of poplar trees. The wealth generated has allowed the family to endow a fine art gallery in the city as well as offering scholarships to Quirm School of Dentistry.

The grandiose Quirm Station, located just outside the Hubwards Gate of the city, could almost be a town hall. It was designed by the famous Quirmian architect Guy d'Nord, and is a tribute to the Epheban style of architecture with a vast portico decorated with carvings of lobsters, scallops and other crustacea.

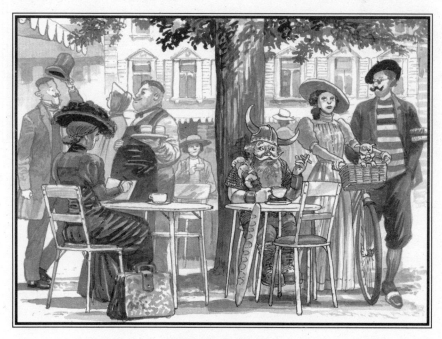

An open carriage or horse bus takes visitors to the city centre; it is a delightful experience to travel along wide tree-lined boulevards with the bright awnings of pavement cafés and ice-cream parlours on either side. A gentle breeze carries with it the aroma of fresh coffee and scent of floral displays mixed with a hint of scallops on the turn and the evocative smell of the pungent tobacco smoked by the local inhabitants.

A visit to Quirm would not be complete without seeing that wonder of horticultural timing, the floral clock, which is located in the Rodley gardens. Plants are selected for the opening and closing times of their blooms which in most cases are accurate to within an hour. Such is the expertise of the Horticultural Research Station here, they receive many requests to provide specimens for floral clocks around the world. Their current project, using the Campanula genus, is the development of an alarm clock for the Knockers Up Association in Pseudopolis.

The Zoological Gardens near by house a large menagerie including elephants from Howondaland who, to the delight of many children, enjoy a daily bathe in the sea.

The Worthe Art Gallery has a permanent exhibition of Da Quirm oil paintings and sketches. There is a fine collection of landscapes as well as some modern sculpture. I must confess to some confusion about a new exhibit entitled 'Avant Gourd' which comprised an unmade bed stacked up with a random and colourful collection of cantaloupe melons and pumpkins. It seemed to me a waste of perfectly good food. Admission to the gallery is free and it is open most afternoons.

The nearby central post office is worth a look for its interesting frieze. In the early days of the postal service, a ducal decree that the mail should be delivered by ostriches was taken at face value by the good burghers of Quirm. By the time they realized that this strange dictum was the result of the duke speaking with his mouth full, the post office building was completed.

Quirm College for Young Ladies, a fine building overlooking

Three Roses Park, is a prestigious educational establishment and numbers among its pupils (aside from this humble author) the children of many notable families, whom it sends out into the world at the end of their schooldays with not only a vigorously developed Moral Fibre but also an excellent back crawl and breaststroke.

On a personal note I was pleased to see that the Fish and Chip Shop in Three Roses Alley is still there. When I was a girl at the college, this was a favourite haunt for many of us, not least because of the handsome young man working behind the counter. I would imagine the good-looking man now in charge is his son.

La Sorbumme, the Fools' Guild summer school and retirement home, is located in the old part of the city adjacent to the site of the collapsed tower. Impromptu and noisy entertainments by silly old fools create quite irksome street theatre in this district and the liberal distribution of banana skins and custard pies may well be the death of some of the elderly folk who have retired here for a quiet life.

It is worth noting that the City Assembly has laid down strict licensing laws. Bars are closed on Octeday and during the rest of the week they normally close before 10.00 in the evening. Quirm is indeed an agreeable city for a vacation, convalescence or retirement.

As yet the seafront is unspoiled and the sandy beaches and little offshore islands are the main attraction of the resort.

Before laying down your picnic blanket on the beach, check for clumps of a kind of seaweed known locally as snapping bladders. This vicious plant, which can move very quickly, will bite the unwary and maliciously kick sand in your picnic. Beware also the shoals of trifle fish that shoot a stream of viscous yellow liquid from their trailing tentacles, which is an annoyance to beachgoers but collected and prized by some Quirmian chefs.

ACCOMMODATION AND REFRESHMENTS

DIMMUCK

THE STATION HOTEL

A newly constructed establishment benefiting from modern hygienic appliances. Its twenty rooms all have comfortable and clean beds. The large dining room serves local fare, and is open all day.

THE COOPER'S ARMS INN

A family-run hostelry offering a friendly service and good breakfasts.

· · · · · · · · · · · · · · · · · · · ·

CHAMPAL

THE CASTLE HOTEL

Occupies a fine old building in the centre of town, and has twelve rooms for guests (three with private bathroom). It boasts a good restaurant (booking required) and residents' bar. Stabling and accommodation for servants is provided.

THE SELACHII ARMS

A large and ancient inn frequented by local farmers and offering a good range of local ciders.

· · · · · · · · · · · · · · · · · · · ·

QUIRM

HOTELS:

THE DUCHY HOTEL, GRAND BOULEVARD

Once the summer residence of Brenda, dowager Duchess of

Quirm, now expanded into a fine hotel but still under her patronage. There are fifteen balconied rooms overlooking the sea, all with private bathroom. The restaurant offers fine dining and an extensive wine list with access to the Rodley carp pools, oyster beds and cellars. Kennelling for swamp dragons available.

THE GRAND HOTEL

Has forty comfortable rooms, many with en suite basins and footbaths.* There is a good grill room and sun-lounge.

THE NEW PAVILION

A recently completed hotel, offers budget accommodation for all the family, with a children's indoor play area in a soundproofed compound. Safe beach (guaranteed free of bladder snappers) with lifeguard on Wednesday.

RESTAURANTS:

SCOFFERS, POMME BOULEVARD

Cutting-edge Quirmian cuisine from Vesta Bloom. Speciality du maison: Seaweed purée with spitty-ceps and aiselle-rolled meatballs.

ALFONSE'S BISTRO, RUE D'ALERT

Good value family restaurant.

GLOWBERRY'S CAFÉ, AVENUE CRAVAT

Traditional and substantial Ankh-Morpork cooking for those missing a taste of home who want food without avec or garlic. Suet puddings a speciality.

For those travellers who would like a more comprehensive guide to Quirm's many restaurants, cafés, hotels and guesthouses we recommend the *Mitchell Inn Guide*, available from station bookshops.

* Thanks to the ablutionary apparatus company of Monsieur Bidet and son.

SCOFFERS
Wines of the Month

DOMAIN DE LA MARE
Trodden hygienically by clean feet.
Estate bottled.

RODLEY BAY RED
A complex sporty wine with hints of tobacco and old socks.

SORBUMME CREEK
A dark ruby wine with a cherry nose.

VIN D'GAR PREMIER CRU
An understated palate with nuances of matches and pickled eggs.

CHATEAU DULUX
A brilliant white wine and a great all-rounder.

HAUT SARSONS
A flinty sharp white with acidic overtones.

JUS DE SCARGOTS
A thick and viscous body with notes of pebble and garlic.

BIN END SALE HILL CUVEE 7A.
A revealing and cheeky wine holding within its aromatic throat fresh hints of damp grass and garden ponds.

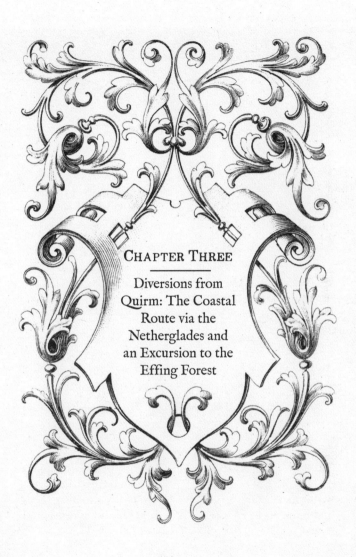

CHAPTER THREE

Diversions from
Quirm: The Coastal
Route via the
Netherglades and
an Excursion to the
Effing Forest

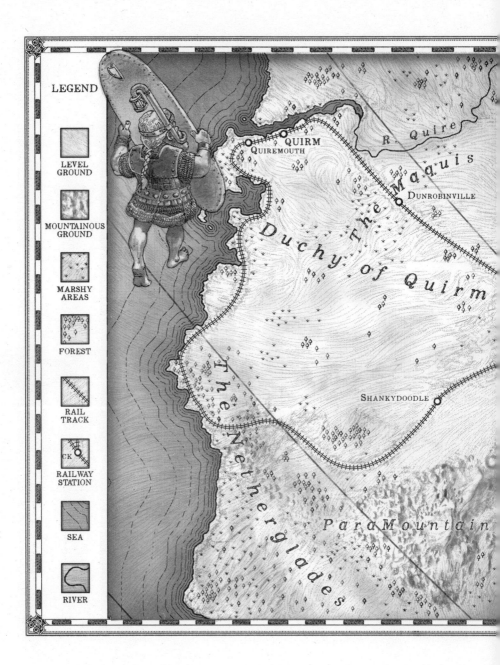

LEGEND

LEVEL GROUND

MOUNTAINOUS GROUND

MARSHY AREAS

FOREST

RAIL TRACK

CK

RAILWAY STATION

SEA

RIVER

QUIRM
QUIREMOUTH

R. Quire

The Maquis

DUNROBINVILLE

Duchy of Quirm

SHANKYDOODLE

The Netherglades

ParaMountain

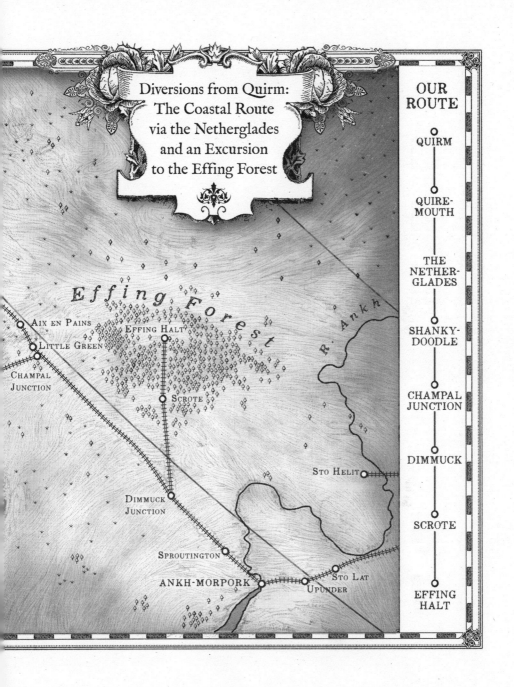

Diversions from Quirm:
The Coastal Route
via the Netherglades
and an Excursion
to the Effing Forest

OUR ROUTE

- QUIRM
- QUIRE-MOUTH
- THE NETHER-GLADES
- SHANKY-DOODLE
- CHAMPAL JUNCTION
- DIMMUCK
- SCROTE
- EFFING HALT

Effing Forest

AIX EN PAINS

EFFING HALT

LITTLE GREEN

CHAMPAL JUNCTION

SCROTE

R. Ankh

STO HELIT

DIMMUCK JUNCTION

SPROUTINGTON

ANKH-MORPORK

UPUNDER

STO LAT

3

The railway line extends from Quirm City to the coast, where it turns back towards Ankh-Morpork via a slow but scenic route. At present the only way to travel further turnwise to Llamedos and beyond is by road or boat. Delays in completing the bridge over the Quire are not the only reason for this. It seems that the city council in Pseudopolis (mainly small shopkeepers with vested interests) assert they 'will have no Ankh-Morpork Kettle fouling their air, frightening their horses and discolouring their sheep's fleeces'. However such is the demand for travel turnwise the AM&SPHR is planning to run a line through the small fishing port of Soarmouth, some miles from Pseudopolis City.

The first stop on the coastal line is the resort of Quiremouth, once a small fishing village, but now becoming a popular day-trip destination. In the summer this train is filled with children clutching buckets and spades, shrimping nets and miniature harpoons; their harassed parents laden with picnic baskets, towels and folding chairs.

There are a few freshly painted guesthouses opening up along the seafront and stalls selling winkles, banged grains and a strange, sticky

confection which looks like a small colourful cloud, its tacky stain evident on the faces and hands of anyone eating it. People do behave in a different way at the seaside: gentlemen roll up their trousers and paddle like small children, while staid matrons, along with giddy girls in service, sport broad-brimmed hats embroidered with a message demanding that they be kissed, and quickly. Troll nannies, slightly comatose from the heat, smile benignly at their charges as they allow sand to be heaped up over their bodies. I have even seen a few dwarfs remove their headgear and expose their bearded faces to the sun. There must be a residual magic in that strand between land and sea.

•QUIREMOUTH•

POPULATION: 120
CLACKS TERMINAL: *on the quay.*
ACCOMMODATION: *Harbour Hotel,
Ship Inn.*
MARKET: *Early morning fish market
on the quay.*
*A small fishing village and seaside
resort on the Quire estuary.*

The slow train from Quire-mouth meanders its way rimwards following the contours of the coast, making occasional stops to take on consignments of fish. Glimpses of blue sea are interspersed with stands of pine trees. On the landward side there are acres of vineyards which produce the famous wines of the region.

The wine makers who live along the coast take advantage of the brief halts where the engine is refuelled or fish is taken on to load their cases of wine into the goods van for delivery to Ankh-Morpork. More often than not, a bottle of their best vintage and a

few glasses find their way into the passenger compartments for a spot of impromptu wine-tasting.

The three-hour journey passes in no time and most travellers are well fortified by the time the train approaches the great steaming swamps of the Netherglades. There is something threatening about this lush green landscape; from the train one can hear raucous birdsong and the buzzing of a thousand mosquitoes - even the sound of train on track changes from *clickety clack* to *thippety thapp* - and the ground trembles as the train passes. Constructing the railway around this area was one of the most difficult engineering challenges of the whole route and it is easy to understand why. Dry land is hard to find anywhere.

A report from one of the surveyors working on the project sheds more light on the Netherglades.

From: Deputy Surveyor Ankh-Morpork-Quirm Line
To: Chief Engineer, AM&SPHR Co.

Dear Sir,

Surveying in the Netherglades was undoubtedly the most difficult task I have ever faced. There was no possibility of draining the land and I'm certain we took the only option by sinking wooden hurdles into the bog and then filling in with earth and boulders.

The climate is torrid and the unique local flora and fauna comprises poisonous and carnivorous plants, shrieking birds, biting mosquitoes the size of hen's eggs and giant black-headed leeches. However, the local inhabitants, who have created rafts on which to live and garden, are not unfriendly, and have provided us with remedies to heal the boils, insect bites, toxic dandruff and squelch foot caused by said wildlife. When I found myself cast down by the whole horrible, heaving, mud-soaked enterprise, a little old man (I knew he was a local because of his webbed feet) approached me with the offer of a potion distilled from a local plant and a promise that it would improve my mood. Within minutes it had an effect and I became absolutely certain in a way I have never been certain before. This certainty stayed with me long enough to resolve the immediate difficulties. I strongly recommend that the AM&SPHR should acquire some of this distillate and make it available to all senior surveyors and engineers. I was told there was a member of the faculty of the Unseen University in the vicinity carrying out research but when I approached him he just ran away leaving behind a worn and very muddy pair of sandals. It might be worthwhile speaking to our contacts at the University for more information.

Yours in absolute certainty

Elias Trim

Leaving the Netherglades the train travels hubwards and resumes its normal speed and rhythm; the climate becomes more temperate and grassy fields dotted with trees extend in every direction. In little over an hour the outskirts of Shankydoodle come into view.

Here white-painted picket fences delineate the fields, and grand mansions with stable yards are much in evidence.

I was told by a fellow traveller, wearing highly polished elastic-sided boots, a tweed jacket over a scarlet waistcoat, and a yellow silk cravat, that Shankydoodle is the most important centre of race-horse breeding in the world; it is from these stud farms that some of the finest thoroughbreds have emerged, including the famous Klatchian Star who won every race he entered until he fell at Hitcher's Ditch and was dispatched to a useful afterlife courtesy of Clancy & Son Pet Supplies.

The station at Shankydoodle is large and well kept, a reflection of the wealth of the inhabitants and the popularity of the racetrack which, thanks to the railway, now draws in thousands of people from as far away as Ankh-Morpork and Quirm.

•SHANKYDOODLE•

POPULATION: 295
CLACKS TERMINALS: *at the railway station and the racecourse.*
POST OFFICE
ACCOMMODATION: *The Turf Club, The White Horse Inn, Captain Pepper's Inn.*
BANK: *Royal Bank of Ankh-Morpork.*

Annual horse fair and horse yearling sales in April.
This area is celebrated for its horse-racing and is also a centre of specialist medical excellence. The small cottage hospital has an Igor who can repair the most complex limb fractures and spinal injuries in both man and horse. NB His stock of spare parts is strictly segregated.

SHANKYDOODLE

RACING CALENDAR FOR THE YEAR OF THE RECIPROCATING LLAMA

15TH MAY, GOLDISH CUP DAY
PRIZE RACE: The Selachii Chase $500

12TH JUNE, DUKE'S DAY
PRIZE RACE: The Rodley Trophy $1000

14TH GRUNE, LADIES DAY
PRIZE RACE: The Euphemia King Gold Medal $500

12TH AUGUST, FAMILY DAY
PRIZE RACE: The Fillies Handicap Prize $100

10TH SPUNE, LAST CHANCE DAY
PRIZE RACE: The Clancy Cup Prize $50

12TH SEKTOBER HARVEST DAY
PRIZE RACE: The Bendigo Runners Cup $250

THE PREMIER ENCLOSURE OFFERS A COVERED GRANDSTAND WITH A VIEW OF THE WINNING-POST. THERE ARE TWO RESTAURANTS (THE FULL COURSE AND GORDON'S ODDS) AND TWO BARS (THE LUCKY HORSESHOE AND MURPHYS).
THE GRAND ENCLOSURE HAS AN OPEN GRANDSTAND, A BAR (THE EACH WAY) AND TWO FOOD OUTLETS OFFERING NAMED-MEAT PIES AND SNACKS.
THE CLANCY ENCLOSURE HAS A STAND AT THE HALFWAY POINT OF THE RACE WITH A GOOD VIEW OF THE RAILWAY.

ALL BETTING STRICTLY LICENSED BY THE GAMBLERS' GUILD.

MRS. WIDGERLY'S LODGER............12/1
Has plenty of stamina, good chance with less weight to carry.

OH FOUR TUNA
.................................93/1
Good on the wet, known biter.

MS. LIZZY'S LAMENT.................2/1
A lovely filly, sure to finish, one to keep an eye on.

MILLION TO ONE
.................................1/1
Strongly fancied, won 9 of the previous 10 entries.

MORTEM CREEK
.................................75/1
Fell at the second last year, could go further.

DUNRUNNIN..295/1
Useful chaser at the King's Meet but got lost on the second. Under-raced.

Even if one is not a follower of the turf, Shankydoodle is a pleasant place to stay. There are several scenic walks through the parkland and it is worth getting up early to see the horses at the morning gallops. One can hear the thunder of their hooves before they emerge from the dawn mists in a rush of speed. Exhilarating indeed.

On race days there is an air of anticipation and excitement in the town. The jostling crowd is a mixture of the wealthy (well-dressed owners in conversation with trainers and jockeys) the hopeful (serious-looking men wearing flat caps and binoculars, intent on their racing paper) and the desperate, those to whom a flutter on the races has, over the years, turned into more of a forlorn flapping with serious consequences to their personal finances. And of course there are day-trippers with a few dollars to risk on the favourite runner. Since gambling is frowned upon in the dwarf fraternity few are in evidence here. On the other hand trolls have embraced the turf with some enthusiasm and troll consortiums now own several racehorses. They have also embraced racing fashions and what appears, at first glance, to be a large, brightly checked tweed marquee is likely to be one or more trolls checking out their investments.

Trolls have brought more than just their huge size and sartorial dash to the turf as is revealed in the attached cutting from the *Shankydoodle Racing Times*.

SHANKYDOODLE

RACING TIMES

12th June, Shankydoodle

RACING CORRESPONDENT NED KITE

As the flag dropped for the start of the $1,000 Rodley Trophy I witnessed the strangest thing. The odds-on favourite runner, Mica Boy, foaming at the mouth, suddenly stopped in his tracks then turned around and attempted to run back along the course while his jockey hung on, helpless to intervene. An enquiry overseen by the Gamblers' Guild released the following statement:

'It is recognized that the unpredictable outcome of horse-racing is not acceptable to the criminal fraternity who employ chemical intervention to enhance an animal's performance. It now seems that the Breccia are also interfering with race results using their own substances, but with the intention of ensuring a very different outcome. One should remember that trolls believe that time is flowing backwards so to them the concept of "The Last Shall Be First" is a better measure of winning than "First Past the Post". On this particular occasion the same horse had apparently been selected to "win" both by Dodgy Derek of the Peaky Gang and by a member of the Breccia, producing the confused activities we witnessed. A consultation has been set up to ensure that this does not happen again.'

The racecourse benefits from a rather fine and somewhat elaborate tote board, originally designed as a five-year desk diary, almanac and appointment device by Bloody Stupid Johnson. Unfortunately its size of over twenty feet by thirty made it impractical and the dates were never correct. The giant device was discovered in a barn close to the racetrack and was renovated by a family of goblins while they lived within its complex interior. With their cooperation the contraption was eventually erected at the main entrance to the viewing paddock where it now displays the time of the races, names of runners and jockeys, the changing odds and for some reason the phases of the moon and high tide in Quirm. It is much admired.

Don't leave Shankydoodle without sampling the local brew, Mudstone's Peculiar, a robust porter made using water from the Netherglades which gives substance to its rich darkness.

The journey continues hubwards, the train passing through a land-scape of pasture and woodland to the usual delays at Champal Junction where it rejoins the main line to Ankh-Morpork.

I once asked Mr Lipwig why the train did not continue back to Ankh-Morpork via the coast. Part of the reason was the difficulty of laying more track through the Netherglades. But the other reason is more curious. Apparently a rival company decided to run a railway along the Circle Sea coast and build a modern holiday resort there. They made good progress for the first hundred or so miles. But then the trouble started and it was reported that workmen on the dawn shift found several pretty girls in filmy clothing tied down to the track who, as the mists lifted, seemed to melt away. There were rumours that these were girls from the Pink Pussycat club, in the pay of the AM&SPHR. Mr Lipwig said he could not possibly comment and that everyone knew the old legends about a place called Holy Wood where a great city disappeared into the sand overnight.

*

From Dimmuck a single-track branch line extends hubwards to Scrote and the Effing Forest. The train has just one carriage for passengers, the rest being flatbed trucks or wagons to transport timber from the forest.

I am told that Scrote hasn't changed much even with the arrival of the railway. A narrow stone building serves as the station master's office, the upper floor acting as a signal box.

•SCROTE•

POPULATION: 120
ACCOMMODATION: *The Jolly Cabbage Inn, Seth's Livery Stables.*
MARKET DAY: *alternate Fridays.*
Sprout Festival on 5th Offle, Scrote and District Agricultural Show last weekend in June.

A typical small farming community on the Sto Plains where they grow mixed brassicas. The Scrote sprout is a variety known for its hardness; even after being boiled for three hours it can still act as catapult ammunition in the continuing fight against the fat and aggressive pigeons which infest this region.

LEVEL AND UNLEVEL CROSSINGS

At the point where the railway meets one of Scrote's two roads the right of way across the junction is governed by a level crossing. Gates close

off the track from the road traffic until a train is approaching, when a bell rings in the station master's office, prompting him to move the gates to bar the road and allow the train free passage.

The system works well here, but elsewhere, according to the guard on the train, the rumour that the purpose of the gates was to indicate a request stop has caused some minor injuries as well as disappointment. Large signs have now been erected at all level crossings explaining their purpose.

NOTICE

AM&SPHR Co. WARNING

• •

DO NOT attempt to cross the line when the gates are closed.

DO NOT leave any cart/carriage/wheelbarrow/perambulator or other wheeled vehicle on the railway track at any time.

DO NOT tether your goat/camel/donkey/horse or indeed any animal or child to the gate at any time.

When the gate is closed, or almost closed, or starting its journey from open to closed, do not climb or vault over it, nor crawl or limbo dance beneath it.

DO NOT borrow, remove, damage or deface any part of the gate.

• •

The AM&SPHR Co. have absolutely no responsibility whatsoever for your person or property if it is on, or adjacent to, the railway track whether or not these gates are open/closed/broken/lost/stolen.

• •

By an accident of geography (or maybe because the surveyors were guests of the hospitable landlord of the Pickled Cabbage pub near Sto Kerrig), one section of railway track on the Sto Kerrig branch line was laid through the Pickled Cabbage's yard, and a level crossing installed. Reuben Sticky, the said landlord, was planning to make sure the gates closed off the track at meal times, thus causing unscheduled stops for the passengers but a lucrative business for himself. What he actually got was a fine from the railway company who then replaced the gate with a permanent structure. His dismayed regulars now have to put up with the noise and smoke of the trains and the additional inconvenience of the conveniences being the other side of the track.

There is also a story about an engine driver in Ohulan Cutash. He was faced with the conundrum of either disobeying company regulations about road crossings where he should sound his whistle on the approach, or encountering the wrath of his old granny who lived near by and said the noise was enough to wake the dead let alone her and her cat. Apparently he made arrangements with local goblins who, when they see his train approaching, flash with mirrors or lamps to another of their number who deals with the gate.

After Scrote the landscape becomes more wooded, and in less than half an hour the train terminates at Effing Halt deep in the bosky shadows of the Effing Forest. There is a well-constructed wooden station and gantries for loading timber and also coal from the small, family-run mines. A plaque on a dented anvil within the station commemorates Jed and Crucible Wesley, local pioneers in the field of steam power for one short, abruptly ended day.

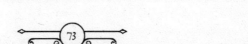

•EFFING HALT•

POPULATION: 41

CLACKS TERMINAL

This stop primarily serves the local logging industry. Most travellers stay in Scrote.

This ancient woodland is home to some interesting flora and fauna: details are recorded in a pamphlet distributed by the Friends of the Effing Forest. This body is now campaigning to save the Effing Great Tit, whose nesting sites are apparently endangered by the greatly increased level of tree-felling. I was shown a copy of a letter they have sent to the railway pleading their cause.

Letter to AM&SPHR Co. from Mrs E. Trellis, secretary to Friends of the Effing Forest Save our Tits Campaign

Dear Sir,

I write to you on behalf of the Friends of the Effing Forest who are greatly concerned by the encroachment upon the forest brought about by those great smoky engines of the railway. Not just the noise they make, nor the clouds of steam, smoke and smuts that now drift into the bosky hollows of our wonderful forest, but the damage that is being

done to the habitat of the Effing Great Tit, a small bird unique to our woodland, by the dreadful depredations that accompany their passage.

The balance of nature is at daily risk as more trees are felled to provide furniture for people who live far away in cities and care not a jot for our wildlife. I myself have seen the loss of more than one hundred nesting boxes that Mrs Pillbeam of the Homes for Little Birds Trust had furnished with her colourful little crocheted squares.

Nature is not to be denied; the home of the tit and warble fly, the little bald vole and rat-tailed squirrel must be protected. I propose a meeting with those in charge of the railway to demand our rights and the rights of all those to whom the forest is a home.

Yours truly,

Evadne Trellis (Mrs)

The Effing Forest is also home to lumberjacks who, it is reported, are often the worse for drink, a most unfortunate condition for young men whose livelihood depends on the axe. Unsurprisingly, there is an Igor Rapid Response Unit based at The Forester's Arms, where impromptu entertainment is sometimes provided by the lumberjacks who have formed a rustic and somewhat energetic choir.

Tucked away in a glade a mile or so from the station is a shrine to Sweevo, the God of Cut Timber.

It takes the form of a carved pine totem pole about twenty feet high and it is still regularly visited by the local woodcutters. There is a superstition that bad luck will follow if a woman witnesses any of the ceremonies surrounding Sweevo. It has been reported that since the arrival of the Igors the offerings of severed limbs have been replaced with carved wooden representations of the same.

ACCOMMODATION AND REFRESHMENTS

QUIREMOUTH

HARBOUR HOTEL
A small, friendly and old-fashioned hotel with ten rooms, some having the benefit of washing facilities. Children and pets welcome.

THE SHIP INN
Reputedly once the haunt of smugglers, now caters largely for the holiday trade. The cavernous cellars are popular with dwarfs and Alfonse's Wine Bar has taken over the traditional snug bar previously favoured by the local fishermen.

BETTY'S FISH AND CHIPS
Betty, originally from Ankh-Morpork, serves generous portions of fresh fish and good chips with bread and butter and a cup of tea. Highly recommended.

· ·

SHANKYDOODLE

THE TURF CLUB
Close to the racecourse, offers superior accommodation and dining to members and their guests. The upper tap room has a fine view of the final furlong.

THE WHITE HORSE INN
Offers good food and comfortable rooms. The large restaurant has a public weighbridge so that jockeys can weigh themselves in and weigh themselves out after a serious steak and kidney pudding.

CAPTAIN PEPPER'S INN
The traditional haunt of the trainers. It was named for the late Captain Pepper who, it is recorded, lost more on the races than anyone else in the town's history. When he retired it was presented to him by a consortium of grateful bookmakers. Accommodation is limited to just two rooms but the all-day breakfast is good value.

. . . .

SCROTE

THE JOLLY CABBAGE INN
A traditional Sto Plains hostelry. There is stabling for horses by arrangement with Seth's Livery Stable and two rooms with shared washing facilities. Food is available using locally sourced ingredients. The bar serves locally brewed cabbage beer and a fortified cabbage wine. Even the locals say it smells a bit cabbagey.

. . . .

THE EFFING FOREST

THE FORESTER'S ARMS
A small inn frequented by woodcutters and miners. The landlord, Mr Forefather, and his wife produce excellent bacon sandwiches.

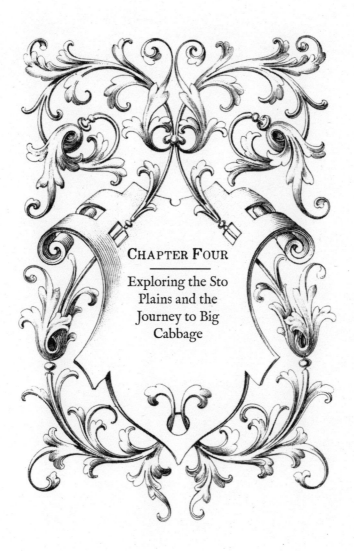

CHAPTER FOUR

Exploring the Sto
Plains and the
Journey to Big
Cabbage

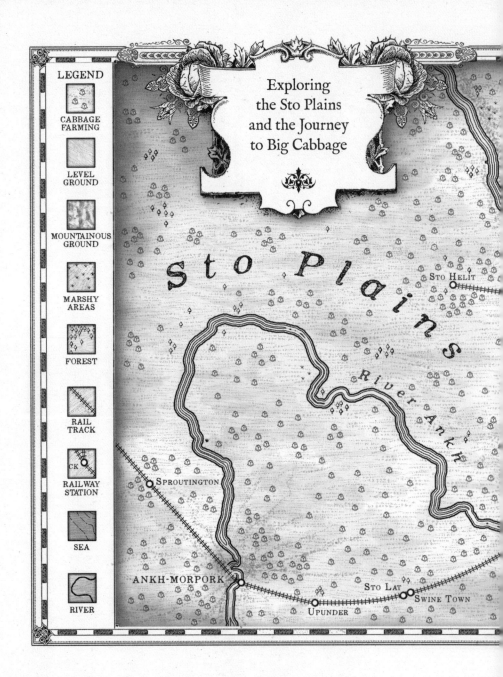

Exploring
the Sto Plains
and the Journey
to Big Cabbage

LEGEND

CABBAGE
FARMING

LEVEL
GROUND

MOUNTAINOUS
GROUND

MARSHY
AREAS

FOREST

RAIL
TRACK

CK

RAILWAY
STATION

SEA

RIVER

Sto Plains

STO HELIT

River Ankh

SPROUTINGTON

ANKH-MORPORK

STO LAT

SWINE TOWN

UPUNDER

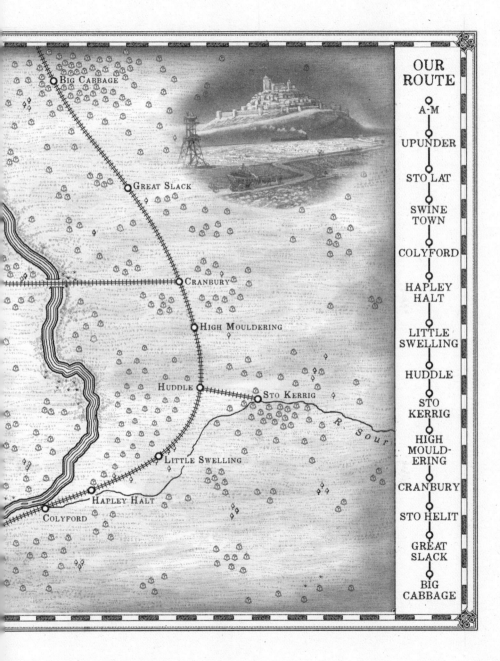

BIG CABBAGE

GREAT SLACK

CRANBURY

HIGH MOULDERING

HUDDLE · STO KERRIG

LITTLE SWELLING

HAPLEY HALT

COLYFORD

R. Sour

OUR
ROUTE

A·M

UPUNDER

STO LAT

SWINE
TOWN

COLYFORD

HAPLEY
HALT

LITTLE
SWELLING

HUDDLE

STO
KERRIG

HIGH
MOULD-
ERING

CRANBURY

STO HELIT

GREAT
SLACK

BIG
CABBAGE

4
—

The single-class stopping train to Big Cabbage leaves from platform 2 of New Ankh Station. This country train is very friendly; everyone seems to know everyone else, as they clamber on at the stations along the line, armed with shopping bags and baskets for the journey to market, or going to see family and friends in the surrounding towns and villages. There are a good number of trolls, generally travelling in their own open carriage, on their way to visit their families in the new housing estates in Sunink. What were once small villages on the outskirts of the city have expanded into suburbs so that the view from the train is rows and rows of new houses which fill the gaps between the old farm buildings. There is a certain similarity to all these houses and it appears that builders will erect a row of dwellings in a week and sell them by the weekend and even arrange for the goods and chattels of the new owners to be delivered by cart before the ink is dry on the contract. Such is the competition between builders that they employ a number of trolls to walk beside the track with huge sandwich boards offering property for sale.

*

About half an hour after leaving Ankh-Morpork, the train stops at the township of Upunder. This once typical Sto Plains community is now home to many families who have moved out from Ankh-Morpork to enjoy the bouquet of the cabbage-enriched air.

•UPUNDER•

POPULATION: 550
CLACKS TERMINAL
POST OFFICE
ACCOMMODATION: *Keevil's Hotel,
The Boot Inn.*
MARKET DAY: *Wednesday.
Squash Monday Fair, third Monday in
June, marks the start of the caterpillar
eradication season.*

Upunder is a small but expanding town with a tradition of cabbage-growing and cobbling. The Offle King cabbage thrives here and its robust outer leaves provide sustainably produced soles for the practical and hard-wearing Upunder boot, which to generations of farmers has meant the difference between being dry-shod and suffering from

Squelch, a nasty fungal affliction brought about by spending one's working life with damp feet amid rotting vegetable matter. Now it seems that some young people have taken to wearing these boots as a fashion accessory, which has led to a trade in inferior imported boots using a cheaper leaf. These are reported to smell dreadfully when wet; so much for progress and the vagaries of fashion.

The endless fields of brassica stretch in every direction with a sameness that might be restful were it not for the overwhelming odour of the cabbage. An hour after leaving Ankh-Morpork the city of Sto Lat appears on the horizon perched on its rocky outcrop like a fortress island on a sea of bilious green. This ancient kingdom had until the coming of the railway more history than future, and is ruled by Her Supreme Majesty Queen Kelirehenna I, Lord of Sto Lat, Protector of the Eight Protectorates and Empress of the Long Thin Debated Piece Hubwards of Sto Kerrig. She has been most forthcoming in her views as to the benefits of the railway to a small kingdom built on the fortunes of leaf vegetables, and was behind the building of the modern terminus outside King Olerve's Gate. It is constructed to look in keeping with the surrounds by employing the artifice of crenellated towers and what appears to be a huge portcullised gate that is in fact the entrance to the engine sheds. Sto Lat Junction, to give it its official name, forms the centre of a network which extends as far hubward as Uberwald, and the great engine sheds and workshops of Swine Town lie near by.

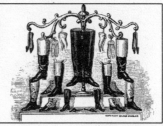

•STO LAT•

POPULATION: 9,800
CLACKS TERMINAL AND GRAND
TRUNK OFFICE
POST OFFICE
ACCOMMODATION: *The Queen's
Head, The Railway Hotel, The
Runcible Arms, The Plough Inn.*
BANKS: *The Cabbage Growers'
Cooperative, Apsley's Commercial.*
MARKET DAYS: *Wednesday and
Saturday.*
*Grand Agricultural Show in May, Soul
Cake Duck Parade in Sektober, Cabbage
Scramble and Rolling contest in Ick.*

Sto Lat is the commercial centre of the cabbage-growing business and boasts the Grand Brassica Exchange Building as well as the Rutabaga Assembly Halls. The Josiah Remnant mural in the latter is reported to be his largest rendition of *Prospect of Sprouts Upon a February Morning.*

The Castle Museum, which is open to the public (daily from ten until four, admission free), houses an interesting collection of double action seed drills, early Humdrummer's single-tine fork dibbers and the complete musical vegetable collection of Aloysius Musk.

The castle gardens have a good display of herbaceous plants and ornamental cabbage. The maze has been closed to the public after complaints that starving visitors trapped inside had to be fed by throwing sandwiches and bits of cake to them from the battlements. It was reported that a family of dwarfs even resorted to tunnelling to make their escape. The maze was planted to a plan provided by that 'master' of landscaping, B. S. Johnson. This plan, preserved in the museum, was drawn on a piece of paper that had also been used to sketch a design for a cruet. Further confusion was added by the many circular coffee stains and part of a note from Mrs J. to her chambermaid.

Sto Lat is well known for its community of skilled blacksmiths and metalworkers who historically used the ore found in the rock that the city is built on. (Legends tell that this isolated crag was carried here from the Ramtops in the days of the Ice Giants.) The local seams

were soon worked out and, until the arrival of the railway, iron ore, along with coal, copper and tin, was brought in by mule-trains in the summer and troll-drawn sleds in the winter. The metalworking industry is now revitalized, although many of the younger craftsmen have migrated to Swine Town where the wages are higher and the only cabbage they see is on a plate. With gravy.

Sto Lat's prestigious Military Academy, located just outside the city walls, still enrols the younger sons of the Sto Plains gentry, although in these peaceful times a career in the Royal Sto Plains Riflers is no longer the reliable source of income, enemy boots and other such spoils of war as it once was.

The cadets spend as many hours learning the intricacies of etiquette as they do military strategy. One may often spy a hapless cadet or two outside, julienning potatoes, polishing oyster forks or performing endless Borogravian Waltz drills as punishment for some infraction.

Travelling the few miles to Swine Town one can usually hear it before one sees it. The sound of mighty hammer presses permeates not just the town but the countryside for some way out, rattling farmhouse windows and causing the ground to tremble. The sound could be mistaken for thunder were it not so regular. The sky above is lit by the red glow of the forges like some crucible of the gods and everything is covered in a fine black dust. There are vast sheds where serious and clever men in oil-stained dungarees create from steel sheet and bar the finely engineered steam machines that

power our railway. Swine Town is a wonder of our age and its whole population is directed towards that one purpose.

•SWINE TOWN•

POPULATION: 690

CLACKS TERMINAL

POST OFFICE

ACCOMMODATION: *The Forge Inn has rooms. As the town expands more public houses, canteens and dormitories are opening up to cater for the vast army of workers. Visitors normally choose to stay in Sto Lat.*

BANK: *Royal Ankh-Morpork Bank.*

The station in Swine Town is functional, surrounded by extensive shunting yards where a continuous stream of trucks deliver iron ore and coal from the quay at Colyford a few miles upriver. Swine Town is a place of pilgrimage for locomotive enthusiasts, who spend their days hanging around writing down engine numbers and other details in little notebooks. Mr Simnel's Aunt Maudie, who runs Simnel's Café just beside the station, also supplies these young men, and it is invariably young men, with that item of hooded waterproof clothing now becoming known as the Anorankh.

•COLYFORD•

POPULATION: 306

CLACKS TERMINAL

POST OFFICE: *Counter in General Store.*

ACCOMMODATION: *The Waterman's Inn, The Cellar Inn.*

MARKET DAY: *Saturday.*

Riverboat Festival in May: a weekend of fun, frolics and sociable crochet, culminating in a parade of decorated boats.

This small settlement on the banks of the River Ankh was once a quiet and somewhat backward town whose river trade comprised mainly wool and cheese coming downriver from Lancre. There used to be a small fish-processing plant where the Ankh green-gilled chub was transformed into something almost edible in a jar. This has recently closed and Colyford is now a bustling river port where the raw materials for building the railway are fed at great speed by the crowds of dockmen from barges on to railway trucks and thence to the forges of Swine Town. There is little else to see but the smell of the town is less offensive than it was and locals can now afford to make their sandwiches with named meat.

The journey hubwards takes us next to the hamlet of Hapley. In Spune there are frequent delays on this line caused by leaves shed by bolting cabbages. Unlike the Blue Bolter, which runs away when startled, the Burley Bolter is classed as an aggressive brassica and will pounce upon a moving object. Burly Bolters are not robust enough to damage engines, but cleaners report that removing the debris from the wheels is a greasy and smelly job. I was told that the AM&SPHR have requested that farmers use the land abutting the railway solely for growing potatoes or some other passive vegetable.

NOTE: The Burly Bolter cabbage was bred by Lord Burleigh, who was endeavouring to develop a new form of cockfighting without killing birds. His Burly Combat sprout has proved impossible to control and it has been reported that some escapes have set seed. A cross between this variety and the Scrote Sprout would I fear be most unwelcome.

•HAPLEY•

POPULATION: 62 1/2
CLACKS TERMINAL: *Nearest is ten miles away at Colyford.*
POST OFFICE: *Counter in Scrimp's General Store.*
ACCOMMODATION: *The Rumptuous Arms.*
MARKET DAY: *Friday.*

Ken Ditch, the founder of the Very Plain Potato church, was born in Hapley and there is still a small shrine in the front room of his parents' terraced cottage in Beehive Lane. There is a small trade in the sale of sacred relics of the founder; these take the shape of wizened and dried-out potatoes that are worn around the neck on baling twine. Some converts have taken to wearing wristbands of the twine alone, like some small scratchy bangle.

Further afield, Rumptuous Hall, a once grand house but now in ruins, was the home of the Rumptuous family.

The unexplained disappearance of the septuagenarian Lord and Lady Rumptuous has never been resolved and their only son, Cuthbert, went missing on an expedition to find the source of the River Z'boozi in Howondaland. Some impression of the former grandeur of the estate may be gained from the famous Remnant painting believed to show the grounds, *Still Life with Cabbage, Broccoli both Green and Purple, Sprouts, Kale and Elderly Couple being Attacked by Werewolf.*

The journey continues with the never-changing view and ever-pleasant aroma of cabbage fields. Even the unassuming railway stations are built to a common plan, with little to raise the interest of the traveller. It is, however, worth getting off at Little Swelling, the acknowledged centre of the worm-herding tradition. The ancient ways of the worm herder had at one point almost died out but, like many things put aside in the name of progress, their work was much missed and regeneration and breeding programmes are now under way. The station master, who is himself an amateur worm breeder of some renown, is also the curator of the small museum and will open it to visitors for a small remuneration. It boasts a fine collection of herder's prongs, travelling trowels, scoops and flat pans as well as the worm-skin tunic and socks worn by fabled worm herder Thaddeus Spelt.

LITTLE
•SWELLING•

POPULATION: 148
CLACKS TERMINAL: *at the Worm Herder's Arms.*
ACCOMMODATION: *The Worm Herder's Arms.*
Annual Worm Races are held in the second week of April on a measured section of platform 1.
The back room of The Worm Herder's Arms is the meeting place for the

Ancient and Alluvial Lodge of the Fraternal Herders Association. The Association offers the use of its secure worm pens and grading riddles free of charge to members.

There is an unusual railway bridge just outside the village. It was constructed to cross King Paragore's Way or, in local parlance, Old Limmer's Gap, an ancient worm-herder's pathway protected not just by custom but by a royal decree. This bridge is unique in that it stands only two foot off the ground, and is maintained by a family of goblins who needless to say have taken full advantage of the transitory resource that passes beneath them.

There is a small shrine to Aniger built into the stone pavement of the bridge. Once a year the low bas relief of a group of flattened animals is scrubbed clean and a small wreath laid.

The post office sells postcards of this curious monument along with a pamphlet containing prayers to Aniger and some tasty recipes for track kill.

•HUDDLE•
(Change here for Sto Kerrig)

POPULATION: 134
CLACKS TERMINAL: *at Huddle Coat Works, New Sheds.*
POST OFFICE: *Counter at Huddle General Stores.*
ACCOMMODATION: *The Huddle Inn.*
MARKET DAY: *Alternate Thursdays. Bud-Harvest Day Fair in February.*

The settlement of Huddle has grown up around the Huddle Inn, an amalgam of three ancient buildings leaning together like old drunkards at closing time. It was until recently the main coaching inn on the road between Sto Kerrig and Big Cabbage.

A viable textile industry has developed here based on the locally grown Cotton-bud Sprout. Skilled weavers make practical waxed jackets, which are both waterproof and mothproof though sadly prone to caterpillar damage.

•STO KERRIG•

POPULATION: 4,400
CLACKS TERMINAL
POST OFFICE: *in the Market Square.*
ACCOMMODATION: *The Crown and Railway Hotel, Coach and Horses Inn.*
BANK: *The Sto Kerrig Mutual.*
MARKET DAYS: *Wednesday and Saturday.*
Kettle and Kale Games in June, Soul Cake Fair in Sektober, Hog-Ringers Fair in October.

Sto Kerrig is an attractive city located on the River Sour, a tributary of the Ankh, which rises in Sourhead Springs on the borders of Skund and winds its way between banks of willow trees across the plains, to join the Ankh near Colyford.

Remnant Hall, birthplace of the famous artist Josiah Remnant, is now a gallery. The Remnant Foundation offers a small bursary to one student a year, chosen by Miss Constance Remnant, the last surviving and somewhat eccentric relative of the great man. The lucky claimant is expected to work in the distinctive Remnant style but utilizing only what can be found in Miss Remnant's compost heap and applying the same to the canvas with cabbage stalks.

Sto Kerrig is the centre of a papermaking industry based on cabbages; artisan craftsmen produce fine watercolour paper from the white-leaved Bockingfield cabbage; and a special gummed paper - the gum impregnated with broccoli juice - is supplied to the Ankh-Morpork Post Office, who use this stock for their popular 50p Sto Plains Cabbage Industry stamp, designed to appeal to the homesick immigrant's *nostalgie de la chou.*

Just outside the city there is an imposing monument commemorating the fallen of the Great Battle of Sto Kerrig in 1642. The story goes that King Olerve the Unready of Sto Lat was eating a bowl of porridge when he was told of yet another encroachment on to his land by an army from Ankh-Morpork. In a fit of rage he rushed to battle shouting for his unwilling and exhausted infantry to follow him. The large equestrian sculpture depicts a horseman armed only with a spoon and lists the names of each combatant who fell in battle. It goes on to explain that after a short rest they all got up and went home.

HIGH •MOULDERING•

POPULATION: 240
CLACKS TERMINAL
ACCOMMODATION: *The Hotel Continental.*
MARKET DAY: *Wednesday.*
Annual Well Undressing in April, when small children and old people are unwrapped from winter's protective layer of goose grease and brown paper prior to a good scrubbing in the beneficial spring.

High Mouldering boasts wonderful salt-water baths from a pleasantly warm spring, and the owner and his wife give hygienic massages to those who would like to enjoy the benefit. Ladies and gentlemen separately, of course; there is nothing here that could be considered insalubrious or that would shock the most delicate of sensibilities.

People wishing to tour the area may be interested in the Sacred Glade of Shock Knee, which deserves to be noticed for its amazing echoes. A short distance away is a shrine to Anoia, patron goddess for people who have difficulty with things stuck in their drawers.

•CRANBURY•

(Change here for Sto Helit)

POPULATION: 420
CLACKS TERMINAL
ACCOMMODATION: *The Plain View Hotel.*
MARKET DAY: *Friday.*
Prick Out Monday in March (the day when cabbage seedlings are thinned out) ends in a procession of the maidens of the town dressed entirely in last year's cabbage leaves. The young men of the town meanwhile play merry japes secreting slugs among their foliage.

Cranbury, once a staging post at the crossroads between the Sto Lat-Big Cabbage and Sto Kerrig-Sto Helit highways, is now a busy station at the junction of two railway lines. Traditionally it was the centre of a home-based cabbage-bottling business; the industrious housewives of the town developed their own recipe to preserve the bright green colour of the fresh vegetable. Cranbury Cabbage was transported by cart as far as Ankh-Morpork and even Ohulan Cutash where it was regarded as a great delicacy. Since the coming of the railway the process has been industrialized and tin cans, produced in Swine Town, arrive ready to be filled and sealed.

En route to Sto Helit, the train passes close to Smirk Hall, home to a rather unpleasant family who once owned vast tracts of land in this area. The dark turrets and ominous buttresses of the great house are visible from the train and there, in forbidding shadows, perhaps lurks the last club-footed member of this clan. They made their money, it is said, by theft and ransom and kept it by only marrying cousins. They lost it on strong drink, cards and snail racing.

•STO HELIT•

POPULATION: 3,500

CLACKS TERMINAL

POST OFFICE

ACCOMMODATION: *The Grand Hotel, The Castle Arms.*

BANK: *Sto Plains Cabbage Growers'.*

MARKET DAY: *Octeday.*

Nip Day, third Friday in August; Soul Cake Duck Cavalcade with illuminated floats and grand costumes in Sektober.

Sto Helit emerges from the evening gloom, its tall and rather forbidding castle dominating the skyline. The city has long outgrown the corsetry of its ancient walls and spreads itself out along fine avenues with shops and cafés. It enjoys something of a provincial reputation for 'class' and genteel living. The principal attraction is the ancient castle; some rooms are open for public viewing for a small consideration. The Long Gallery holds some fine landscape paintings in the Brindisian style as well as portraits of the Sto Helit ducal family. Lady travellers might

wish to visit Bilberry's Emporium, a most fashionable outfitters with a long tradition of dressing royal families. Their lace-makers and seamstresses created a delightful wedding dress for Queen Magrat of Lancre.

•GREAT SLACK•

POPULATION: 43
CLACKS TERMINAL
POST OFFICE: *counter in Bitlidder's General Store*
MARKET DAY: *Tuesday.*
The Ember String Fair includes a tug of war, and children's knotting games. The fair is regarded as a success if all the children are cut free before dusk.

A small hamlet that tries hard to be bigger, its only interesting feature being a monument to Antipater Slack, grower of the first self-protecting cabbage. This was the Slack Snapper, which devoured all insects that came within reach, thus precluding any possibility of pollination. Perceiving it was in danger of dying out, Antipater worked the field with a small camel-hair paintbrush to do the job himself. Neighbours were later able to trace his passage by those plants that successfully went to seed and his end by the remnants of his clothing and one rubber boot.

The modern descendants of Antipater's plants, now somewhat pacified, yield leaves so strong their fibres can be twisted into robust twine. Great Slack twine is much favoured by farmers and stockmen and is the best cash crop this community has ever had. The sixty-foot-long twine walk may be worth a visit if it's raining.

Big Cabbage's Big Cabbage is visible from several miles away, rising above the flat fields of brassica that surround it like an enormous prize horticultural specimen. From a distance it looks remarkably realistic, but as the train approaches it is possible to see a large door in what is a crude and badly painted concrete structure. The new station is, in contrast, very smart, the woodwork and benches finished in a bright green paint and the station sign decorated with every possible species of brassica. It is a short walk from the station to the amusement park and a regular coach service takes visitors to the modern agricultural centre.

•BIG CABBAGE•

POPULATION: 830

CLACKS TERMINAL

POST OFFICE

ACCOMMODATION: *The Green Crown, The Railway Hotel, Furby's Family Hotel and Camp Site.*

BANK: *Bank of Big Cabbage, Sto Lat.*

BRASSICA MARKET: *daily.*

The Grand Cabbage and Sprout Fair, 1st–3rd Sektober, includes finals of the Sto Plains Cabbage Queen competition; cabbage futures bought and sold. The Big Cabbage Carnival of Kale takes place on 5th Ember.

Big Cabbage, the green heart of the Sto Plains, is a centre of horticultural excellence as well as providing a fun day out for farming families.

Big Cabbage is totally dedicated to the brassica in all its wonderful manifestations. Over the years it has developed from the original Cabbage Growers' Association offices and model farm to become the world centre for training as well as research and development and is, in many ways, a foliate university.

It holds the archive seed collection for not just the Sto Plains, but places as far flung as Lancre and Genua, and there are now 'state of the art' holding pens and grading systems for worms. The Department for Biological Pest Control recently released the results of a landmark investigation into the decline in insect infestations on land near to clacks terminals, concluding that this was

not, as first thought, the effect of strange rays emanating from the machinery, but the simple result of the many goblins who are now so efficiently employed in operating the system augmenting their diet.

A vast amusement park has been built up around the scientific centre to provide entertainment for the families of visiting farmers and this is now the main attraction for the hundreds of day-trippers, eclipsing even the Museum of Caterpillars. The old concrete Big Cabbage acts as a visitor centre and various fairground rides provide refreshment and relentless merriment for all.

ACCOMMODATION AND REFRESHMENTS

UPUNDER

Keevil's Hotel

Situated in the market square is a well-maintained modern hotel offering clean rooms and wholesome and inexpensive food. There are fifteen rooms, most with wash-hand basin and running water. Ground-floor annexe provides accommodation for trolls.

The Boot Inn

A welcoming coaching inn which boasts a fine collection of historic boots and shoes arranged along the beams, in alcoves, and on any other available surface.

Accommodation is limited to two family rooms but the dining room has a good menu of traditional Ankh-Morpork cuisine.

STO LAT

The Queen's Head

The oldest hostelry in the city, full of ancient timbers, inglenook fireplaces and seriously sloping floors. The fine cellar more than makes up for the rather cramped accommodation.

The Railway Hotel

A modern brick-built edifice.

The thirty rooms are clean and well appointed. Porter service to the station is available for travellers in transit. Reinforced accommodation for trolls, cellar rooms for dwarfs.

THE RUNCIBLE ARMS
Once a traditional coaching inn but now under new management. Miss Hubble runs a very comfortable establishment with ten rooms. A profusion of gathered-lace curtains, small china ornaments and whatnots tend to hamper one's progress in the public rooms but otherwise it is a pleasant enough place to stay.

THE PLOUGH INN
A modest concern catering mainly for the local population, serving only snacks and ales.

COLYFORD
THE WATERMAN'S INN
This is an established riverside hostelry unfortunately prone to flooding. For this reason I would recommend the first-floor rooms which have the added benefit of a pleasant river view. Good dining, but I have heard complaints of watery beer.

THE CELLAR INN
The inn is run by a retired dwarf metalworker. Specializing in a river-rat cuisine and quaffable ales, it appeals to the transient dwarf population, who also appreciate the low-ceilinged basement rooms.

HAPLEY
THE RUMPTUOUS ARMS
A small, run-down inn patronized by the local inebriates. It offers simple food and a range of potato-based beers and spirits.

LITTLE SWELLING
THE WORM HERDER'S ARMS
Favoured by passing drovers, since it has its own secure and deep-loam worm pens. Accommodation is fairly basic but very good value, and it is also popular with visitors to the local museum and surrounding attractions.

HUDDLE

The Huddle Inn

A large coaching inn which looks, from the outside, in need of some repair. However with ten well-appointed bedrooms and a pleasant dining room it is an agreeable place to stay.

STO KERRIG

The Crown and Railway Hotel

Offers good accommodation with the advantage of modern plumbing. Like other railway hotels the large dining room offers hot food all day. The ingenuity of the paper-makers of the town is well known, but on a personal note I think the 'recycled tissue' on offer in the ladies' room needs a bit more refinement.

The Coach and Horses Inn

In the centre of town, a regular meeting place on market day. Its six bedrooms all have traditional four-poster beds and coal fires in winter, making it cosy if a little old fashioned. The long walk to the outside privy detracts considerably from its amenity.

HIGH MOULDERING

The Hotel Continental

Offers accommodation tailored for trolls, humans, dwarfs and goblins; fifty rooms are available at present. Combined with a visit to the local spa it provides a welcome break for the tired at weekends, with excellent meals. Highly recommended.

CRANBURY

The Plain View Hotel

Recently purchased by the railway company, this establishment has been comprehensively refurbished to provide multispecies accommodation and all modern facilities.

STO HELIT

The Grand Hotel

Stands head and shoulders above the many other hostelries and inns in this old city. With fifty en suite rooms, a magnificent ballroom hosting daily tea dances and a grand restaurant offering fine Quirmian wines and modern cuisine, it is indeed a luxurious place to stay.

THE CASTLE ARMS

Occupies a fine stone building near the castle that was, in olden times, the city prison. Now much renovated it offers, on the first floor, twelve comfortable rooms. The small, dark ground-floor rooms are favoured by the dwarf fraternity who feel particularly at home here, and appreciate the barred windows not just for their decorative quality but for the security they provide when gold is part of one's luggage. Stories are told of hauntings by headless men and noseless women.

. . . .

BIG CABBAGE

THE GREEN CROWN HOTEL

This is the favoured venue for meetings, whether it's the annual Hogswatch get-together of seed salesmen or an international scientific conference. Offering plentiful and modern accommodation and large public rooms, it occupies an ideal location in the heart of the town. The modern hotel bar claims to serve more varieties of cabbage wine and brassica distillations than any other establishment in the world. The grand dining room, with its wallpaper flocked in a cabbage motif, fine china decorated with cabbages and silver broccoli-shaped cruets, pays homage to the importance of the brassica family to this part of the world.

THE RAILWAY HOTEL

Just completed, and the largest of its type that I have seen in my travels. There is a spacious public drawing room with comfortable seating and children's play area. The hotel runs a daily coach service to the amusement park.

FURBY'S FAMILY HOTEL AND CAMP SITE

Offers good-value family accommodation for all species. Its proximity to the amusement park and Furby's own 'Castle of Cabbage' play area makes it a popular resort. The accommodation is fairly basic.

I append herewith, for those who might be interested, my grandmother's own recipe for Cabbage Soup, a true representation of Sto Plains cuisine.

Take four cabbages (preferably of the 'Jolly Giant' variety, though the 'Kendle Green' will make a suitable substitute). Chop the cabbage small and put in a large pot with three pig cheeks and one pig knuckle per person. Add two pounds of potatoes and six whole onions. Fill pot with water, add a handful of salt and bring to the boil. Simmer for fifteen hours, skimming occasionally.

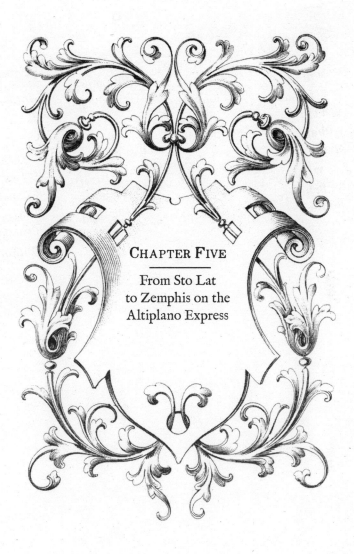

Chapter Five

From Sto Lat
to Zemphis on the
Altiplano Express

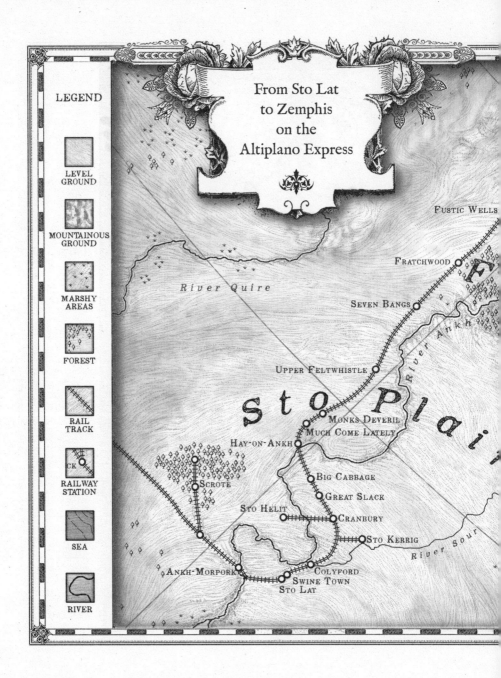

LEGEND

LEVEL GROUND

MOUNTAINOUS GROUND

MARSHY AREAS

FOREST

RAIL TRACK

CK
RAILWAY STATION

SEA

RIVER

From Sto Lat
to Zemphis
on the
Altiplano Express

FUSTIC WELLS

FRATCHWOOD

River Quire

SEVEN BANGS

River Ankh

UPPER FELTWHISTLE

S t o   P l a i

MONKS DEVERIL
MUCH COME LATELY

HAY-ON-ANKH

BIG CABBAGE

SCROTE

GREAT SLACK

STO HELIT

CRANBURY

STO KERRIG

River Sour

COLYFORD

ANKH-MORPORK

SWINE TOWN
STO LAT

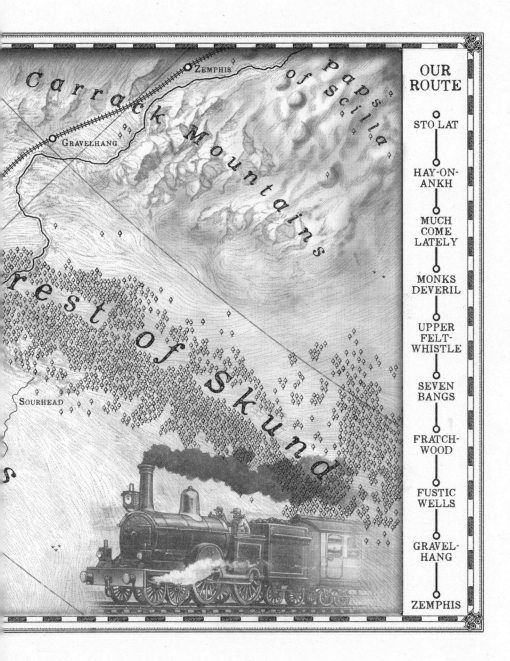

ZEMPHIS

Carrack Mountains

papsila of sciila

GRAVELHANG

rest of skund

SOURHEAD

OUR ROUTE

STO LAT

HAY-ON-ANKH

MUCH COME LATELY

MONKS DEVERIL

UPPER FELT-WHISTLE

SEVEN BANGS

FRATCH-WOOD

FUSTIC WELLS

GRAVEL-HANG

ZEMPHIS

5

Travellers in search of exotic destinations aboard the train may take the Altiplano Express, which starts its long journey hubwards from Sto Lat Junction. A ticket guarantees a private sleeping compartment for the trip as well as a good breakfast in the restaurant car.

I have previously detailed the exterior design of the station, but the interior of this edifice is no less impressive. However, I must say that the numerous arches and columns placed in a seemingly random arrangement present serious obstacles to the troll porters with their luggage trolleys, and the fortifications around the booking office make it almost inaccessible.

The Altiplano Express leaves at eight in the morning from platform 1 which, once you have found your way there, offers a welcome refuge in the form of the fragrant aroma of a coffee shop. Miss Painsworth dispenses exceedingly good coffee in her comfortable and hospitable establishment. The passengers, many of them trolls and dwarfs who are visiting their families back home in Uberwald, gather in groups on the platform beside their allocated carriages. The railway company accommodates dwarfs in special two-tier carriages with heavy blinds at the windows. Families of

trolls pile on to their special reinforced flatbed carriage located behind the engine and tender. They pay a premium to be located here where they can inhale the rich mix of sparks, swirling smoke and smuts which to them is an airborne treat. I suppose to us it might be like being in a shower of biscuits.

This train also has a very large and well-protected mail coach. On my visit there were crates clearly marked 'Igor to Igor' being trollhandled on board, some audibly sloshing despite the 'Handle with Care' stickers which were pasted all over them. The troll porters were also, rather more cautiously, loading a large sarcophagus into a windowless carriage at the rear of the train; this was accompanied by an Igor in full morning dress. As I understand it only black-ribbon vampires are permitted to travel on the railway and I imagine the document that the Igor was proffering to the guard was some proof of compliance. But how could they be sure? Happily the sleeping compartments are located at the front of the train.

The new Railway Watch guard this train. They are well-armed men

wearing the Ankh-Morpork coat of arms and the railway cipher over their smart uniforms. In my experience there is little or no crime on a train journey unless you fall in with a bad lot and play games of chance such as dice or Cripple Mr Onion with kind-looking gentlemen who have lazy eyes and quick fingers. However, additional risks apply on this route, as it passes through the Carrack Mountains and beyond, traditionally a haunt of bandits and highwaymen. Reports in the *Ankh-Morpork Times* tell alarming stories about bandits who block the track with boulders and extort money from travellers. It was a relief to note that all the windows of the sleeping carriage had strong metal shutters. The compartment, though small, contains everything a person might need for a long journey. In addition to a comfortable bed there is a small washbasin with running water, and adequate storage for clothes and hats.

The journey to Big Cabbage is speedy and, with the exception of a couple of brief halts to take on coal and water, non-stop. Half an hour hubwards of Big Cabbage the train crosses the new bridge over the River Ankh. The bridge is guarded by a troll wearing a large red rosette; it seems that he was this year's winner of the Best Kept Bridge Award. The main purpose of this competition is of course to encourage good structural maintenance of the track and bridges, but the contest has revealed a somewhat surprising aspect of troll nature. Many have enhanced their environment with flowering plants, water features and elaborate collages of shells and interesting shales. Sadly it has been found necessary to introduce certain regulations governing these decorative extravaganzas as they are in danger of encroaching on the track, defeating the original purpose of the challenge.

•HAY-ON-ANKH•

POPULATION: 450
CLACKS TERMINAL
ACCOMMODATION: *The Swan Inn,*
Horneyold Arms.
MARKET DAY: *Tuesday.*
Annual Regatta in June, Duck race the
second Octeday in Spune.
A pretty riverside town popular for
fishing and boating holidays.

On the far side of this bridge is Hay-on-Ankh, a small riverside town that has caught a touch of gentility from the numerous 'dressed for boating' visitors who travel on the railway for a weekend of messing about in the river. The original residents, horny-handed fisherfolk who had for generations stood waist-deep in ice-cold water netting coy carp and rimbow trout for little return, other than occupational rheumatics, soon realized that they could rent out their boats and rods and go to the pub instead.

The annual Hay-on-Ankh Regatta attracts visitors from all across the Sto Plains and crews of oarsmen race one another for the Ankh Challenge Cup and the Sto Helit Gold Medal. Sometimes in the heat of the summer this contest is interrupted as families of trolls take to the chilly waters to cool down, creating currents and whirlpools in the stream and causing the scullers to lose their oars or even capsize.

As the line of the railway takes the train away from the river the landscape reverts to cabbage fields, now interspersed with fields of grain and some livestock.

MUCH COME •LATELY•

POPULATION: 330
CLACKS TERMINAL
ACCOMMODATION: *The Snod Bonnet.*
MARKET DAY: *Saturday.*
May Day Pole-Dance in May or Grune.

The well-kept village of Much Come Lately, about twenty-five miles hubwards, is the centre of a thriving hat and bonnet trade. It has a rather fine market monument in the form of an ancient carved pole, around which I'm told the village maidens dance upon the first May day without rain, even if that falls in Grune. The young women display their fitness, flexibility and strength by hanging from this pole in various postures to impress the young men of the village. There is a cream and jelly tea for all participants afterwards.

The folk of Much Come Lately still make the traditional cabbage-stalker hats which have long been employed to protect farm workers from the elements and, at the end of the day, can provide a nourishing soup.

The area between Much Come Lately and Monks Deveril is very pretty with gentle green undulations, small copses, fields of cows and hedgerows trailing streamers of Purple Bindweed and Climbing Henry in the wake of the train.

Much of this land was once part of a monastery, largely demolished by the first Lord Deveril, who was granted the land by King Veltrik III. No record remains of the monks but the water from the well is still believed, by the villagers, to cure dandruff and the palsy.

MONKS •DEVERIL•

POPULATION: 167
CLACKS TERMINAL
ACCOMMODATION: *The Deveril Arms.*
MARKET DAY: *Wednesday.*
Soul Cake Duck garden fête in Sektober.

Deveril Hall is a fine old manor house with spiral, spined bell tower and imposing façade. The gatehouse is built in the style of a Klatchian tent and was constructed after the fifth Lord Deveril had returned from that land of desert and mystery some hundred years ago. However, it is the huge hedge which is truly amazing. It would seem that the seventh Lord Deveril suffered from severe agoraphobia. He had a wild-box hedge planted that occluded the view from every one of his windows and which extended down the drive so that he could take the air without, as it were, being in it. When his son inherited the estate he employed

the young dwarf gardener Modd Modossonsson to turn the hedge into something less oppressive. Given a free hand this keen young horticulturalist proceeded to create one of the growing wonders of the county, a work of unimaginable topiary depicting the whole of the battle of Koom Valley. He enlisted the help of his six brothers, who by dint of using throwing axes for the tall bits had, within a few weeks, sketched out the whole concept in living hedge. The undertaking was not without its problems, the least of which was the decapitation of any number of pigeons, several dozen squirrels and two peacocks. More serious were the injuries inflicted on a junior footman. Of course, being a living plant the hedge requires constant trimming, and no sooner do they get to the far end than they have to start again at the beginning. It is a condition of entry that, if you wish to visit this remarkable achievement, you don a steel helmet, available from the gatekeeper for a modest rental.

UPPER •FELTWHISTLE•

including Lower Feltwhistle and Middle Feltwhistle

POPULATION: 432
CLACKS TERMINAL: *in Upper Feltwhistle.*
ACCOMMODATION: *The Pig Borer's Tale.*
MARKET DAYS: *Wednesday and Friday.*

Annual Pig-Rolling Race last Saturday in Ember.

The train next passes through the Feltwhistles, a group of three small villages merged into one. This enclave is home to the Feltwhistle Peculiar, a pig unique to the area. Being bred for bacon, the characteristics of the animal are its extreme fatness and the shortness of its legs, which also enable it to be rolled to market.

There is of course an annual pig-rolling race down Whistle Hill, and it is rumoured that some wags take it to the extreme and roll their wives as well. The local hostelry is named for the traditional skill of pig-boring, a humane if protracted alternative to the knife. A champion pig borer has his or her own collection of tediously boring tales which could cause the unwary listener to lose the will to live. The plump ladies of the town serve very tasty rolled bacon rolls on the station.

The fields of cabbages return, stretching away on all sides as far as the eye can see, until the train slows for a refuelling stop at Seven Bangs.

SEVEN BANGS •HALT•

(SEVEN BHANGS)

POPULATION: 27
A REFUELLING STOP
HOSTELRY: *The Jolly ~~Green Cabbage~~ Dragon.*

It is hard to know what to make of the blackened deep craters visible from the small station here.

An elderly local on the station platform regales the stranger with tales of a fire-breathing dragon and then tries to sell the unwary travellers what he describes as dragon detectors, which are nothing more than sooty bits of kindling. The real story, though unlikely, is far more mundane. The B'hang family, having heard stories about the endless fields of lush green cabbages of this land, migrated here from the Counterweight Continent in order to produce industrial quantities of the Agatean delicacy called Grimchi, a preserve of fermented cabbage. They harvested their crop of the Jolly Giant cabbage variety, chopped it up and added the local, rather watery, pickling vinegar and their own special seven-spice-black-powder. They then stored this mixture, as was traditional, in giant ceramic pickling jars buried in deep pits. A characteristic of the Jolly Giant cabbage, which every soup-making Sto Plains housewife knows, is that when water is added there is a three hundred per cent increase in volume. The first explosion set up a chain reaction, filling the air with shards of pottery, and great gobbets of foul-smelling sludge, and creating the deep craters we still see. The B'hang family moved swiftly on, as did most of the villagers, afraid that there might still be undiscovered jars fermenting away. Such was the disturbance to the underlying strata that the railway engineers specified the building of extra deep foundations under the track to prevent subsidence and in case of further explosions.

After about an hour the horizon darkens as the Forest of Skund comes into view. The deepest, darkest part of this extensive and sinister woodland extends widdershins of the River Ankh but its turnwise fringes come within a few miles of the railway and this is where the village of Fratchwood is located.

•FRATCHWOOD•

POPULATION: 150
NEAREST CLACKS: *at Seven Bangs*
ACCOMMODATION: *Woodcutter's Arms.*
MARKET DAY: *Tuesday.*
Kindling Thursday Fair, mid Ember.
A small village at the edge of the Forest of Skund reliant on furniture-making and charcoal burning.

The Woodcutter's Arms, which is the only hostelry in the area, is known to the locals as 'Finger Jack's' after a previous landlord, who kept all his fingers, somewhat unusually, in a jar behind the bar. The ones he used were loaned him by an Igor and it would appear they came from the hands of someone quite refined because they fluttered in alarm every time he uttered an oath and insisted he washed them after visiting the privy. There were rumours that he watered his beer and a very unpleasant conclusion was drawn after he was seen to wash his hands every time he came out from the beer cellar carrying a fresh barrel for behind the bar.

Now under new management, the Woodcutter's Arms is almost famous as the retailer of the 'Fratchwood bodged chairs' that have long been a tradition in these parts. They are sold from the old stables where the chairs are penned to prevent them wandering off. Not far away is one of the small forest glades where chair-bodging still goes on. This ancient craft is carried out on 'pole lathes' that are powered by the spring action of a still growing sapling and a hearty stamp of the operative's right leg. The results are surprisingly well finished; chair legs, arms, stretchers and back rails all go off in huge bundles to the 'buttick and basher' who makes the seat and finishes the construction. One can, if one has the time, order a chair with the seat 'made to measure' for one's own posterior. These are said to be remarkably comfortable but

they do have one slight drawback. Fratchwood timber is harvested from the trees of the enchanted Forest of Skund. It is not in any way in the same league as the famed Sapient Pearwood, but it does tend to move about a bit, on its own, when you are least expecting it. Little can be made from this wood that is not firmly nailed to the floor - or fastened to something else substantial. The 'Fratchwood bodged chair' is an exception as it generally only moves away from

fire and sometimes incontinent dogs. It will, I'm told, shuffle up behind you and, if it likes you, nudge the backs of your knees and wait for you to sit down. The chairs don't move very fast and this tendency usually fades as the wood ages and dries out.

The Carrack Mountains are clearly visible on the horizon as the train approaches Fustic Wells, the next station stop, located at the foot of a shallow escarpment.

•FUSTIC WELLS•

POPULATION: 370
CLACKS TERMINAL
ACCOMMODATION: *The Majestic Hotel.*
MARKET DAY: *Wednesday.*
Dipping Day Fair in Sektober.
A small spa town where the particular quality of the waters has been found effective in treating all foot-related ailments.

Once an obscure village with an odiferous spring, Fustic Wells has now developed into a much frequented spa. The yellow-stained waters originally used by trolls as a drench to encourage the growth of beneficial lichens were found to have some efficacy in the treatment of human foot ailments, and several local matrons came forward who had taught themselves podiatry as something to occupy the long winter evenings.

In the new grandiose pump room built of concrete but fronted by a façade of Ephebian-style columns, mature and well-

upholstered women in white coats, wearing stout rubber gloves, wait by their slipper baths, foot wells, heel sinks and toe basins ready to tend the weary traveller's feet.

Fustic Cake is a local speciality reputedly made using spring water. It is a bright yellow, curiously textured confection which is supposed to taste like seed cake. Alas, it does not taste like any seed cake I have eaten.

The gradient increases as the train winds its way ever higher into the mountains. After so long on the plains the air feels fresh and sharp and the scenery is dramatic. One can see, in the valley below, the River Ankh threading its way down to the plains. Ahead, the bright white scars in the rock face indicate that the train is approaching the Gravelhang Quarry stop. This is just a station and sidings that serve a small quarry in which a few families chip a living from the calcareous rocks. Once widely used by sculptors and masons - and in vast quantities - the Carrack marble is here almost exhausted, due in no small part to the construction of the Royal Bank of Ankh-Morpork, in which no wood, paint or indeed cushions were employed if marble could do instead.

•GRAVELHANG•

POPULATION: 45
CLACKS TERMINAL
Site of a small quarry producing prime Carrack marble.

Gravelhang has no inns, no public buildings, and one small general store that sells only canned food, tobacco and banjo strings.

There is now, due to its geographical position only, a clacks relay station here. Wisely the Grand Trunk have insisted that only men used to long service in bad stations operate this relay, and no goblins are allowed. The former might it is supposed

eventually enlarge the gene pool and the latter would get eaten, though this might be the other way round. There is some dispute over that in the Grand Trunk Species Resources department.

The train continues its climb into the Carrack Mountains through the night, eventually coasting gently down into Zemphis as the sun rises.

•ZEMPHIS•

POPULATION: 780
CLACKS TERMINAL: *at the station.*
ACCOMMODATION: *The Station Hotel.*
Modern Zemphis is a lawless and dangerous place for any but the most experienced and well-armed traveller.

This ancient city, its high stone walls visible for miles around, is located at the junction of three trade routes as well as the river route to Ankh-Morpork. In times past the vast central square held a great covered market where traders bought and sold precious metals from the Ramtops, wool from Lancre, coffee, spices and silk from Klatch, as well as the produce of the Sto Plains. Merchants from all over the world settled here creating a wealthy if transient cosmopolitan community. Sadly those days are gone and modern Zemphis has become a place where everything and everyone has a price. The friendly hubbub of international commerce with its many tongues has been replaced with something more akin to a local bazaar; the high-earning cross-border trade is now mainly in contraband such as adulterated treacle, raw Slab and undomesticated imps, and the only common languages that the dealers understand are money and the knife. Travellers are strongly advised not to venture into the city unescorted, and anyone tempted to explore the ruins of Downsized Abbey (now a souk) does so entirely at their own risk.

Even Zemphis Station is very different from anywhere else we've been, and it has a foreign smell of

strong goat's cheese and Klatchian cigarettes. The main concourse is full of small-time traders, a few displaying silk carpets (some seemingly of the flying variety). The railway guards chase away the many unlicensed beggars who have moved here from Ankh-Morpork to dodge the Beggars' Guild rules and rates, and to ply their oozing trade wherever they can find a nook or cranny to slump into.

There is, however, one excursion that I can more safely recommend to the visitor determined to see something of this exotic corner of 'foreign parts': the famous Zemphis Falls.

The traditional viewing point for the falls is a little way outside the city. Here the waters plummet one hundred and fifty feet from the clifftop high above into the foaming river below. The spray hangs in the air, creating rainbows, and a watery mist lies over ancient stone arches and doorways like tissue paper. It is a memorable vision and after twenty-four hours in the train a welcome and refreshing break.

ACCOMMODATION AND REFRESHMENTS

HAY-ON-ANKH

THE SWAN INN

The inn has been recently modernized and the twenty bedrooms all have wash-hand basins with running hot and cold water. The large restaurant offers freshly cooked fish and a well-stocked cellar, and is bedecked with sculling trophies.

THE HORNEYOLD ARMS

The haunt of the local fishermen and boat-builders. Good beer and cider.

• •

MUCH COME LATELY

THE SNOD BONNET

A small inn with just three rooms, all of which are well furnished. Good-value home-cooked meals are available.

• •

MONKS DEVERIL

THE DEVERIL ARMS

Run by an elderly gentleman with a fund of stories about the Deveril family. Accommodation is limited to just two family rooms, both of which are very well appointed if a little old-fashioned. The proprietor's wife, who used to work in the estate kitchen, provides generous helpings of traditional Sto Plains food and particularly delicious Figgins, apparently a favourite of the seventh Lord Deveril. She also makes very good Slow but Sure Gin.

• •

FELTWHISTLE

THE PIG BORER'S TALE

The inn is a large and welcoming hostelry. The well-cooked meals make full use of the Feltwhistle pig: the boiled-bacon and cabbage pie is particularly fine, as are the honey-roast ham meringues.

• •

SEVEN BANGS

THE JOLLY ~~GREEN CABBAGE~~ DRAGON

Not recommended. There is a small bar offering a local cabbage ale which is probably preferable to the water.

• •

FRATCHWOOD

THE WOODCUTTER'S ARMS

This ancient inn on the fringes of the Forest of Skund is surprisingly bright and cheerful and offers good all-day breakfasts and home-made soups. The accommodation is comfortable and it is rumoured that a Fratchwood bed will rock you to sleep.

FUSTIC WELLS

THE MAJESTIC

Built to accommodate visitors to the Springs, the hotel is less majestic than it appears from the façade. However, the twenty bedrooms are clean and bright and all have small private bathroom attached. The spacious dining room has a good menu and the bar is large with comfortable armchairs and a good selection of wines and spirits.

ZEMPHIS

THE STATION HOTEL

Like all AM&SPHR Co. hotels, it is modern and comfortable with well-appointed bedrooms and a restaurant. Cellar apartments are available for dwarfs and there is a troll annexe with bar.

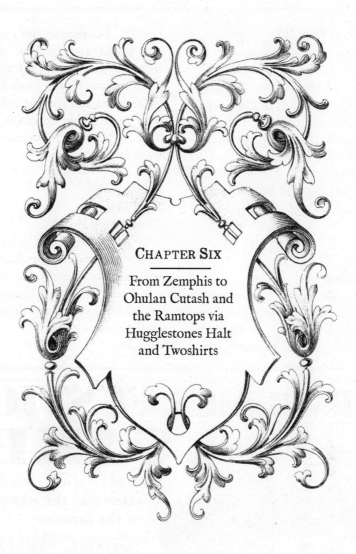

CHAPTER SIX

From Zemphis to
Ohulan Cutash and
the Ramtops via
Hugglestones Halt
and Twoshirts

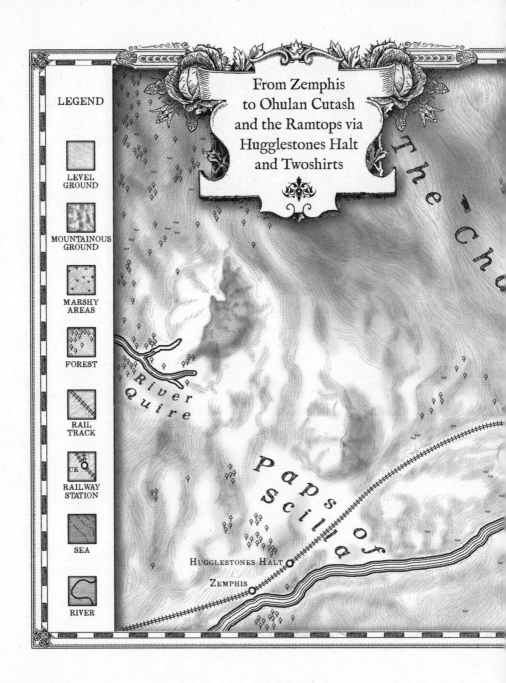

From Zemphis
to Ohulan Cutash
and the Ramtops via
Hugglestones Halt
and Twoshirts

LEGEND

LEVEL
GROUND

MOUNTAINOUS
GROUND

MARSHY
AREAS

FOREST

RAIL
TRACK

CK

RAILWAY
STATION

SEA

RIVER

River Quire

The Ch...

Paps of Scilla

HUGGLESTONES HALT

ZEMPHIS

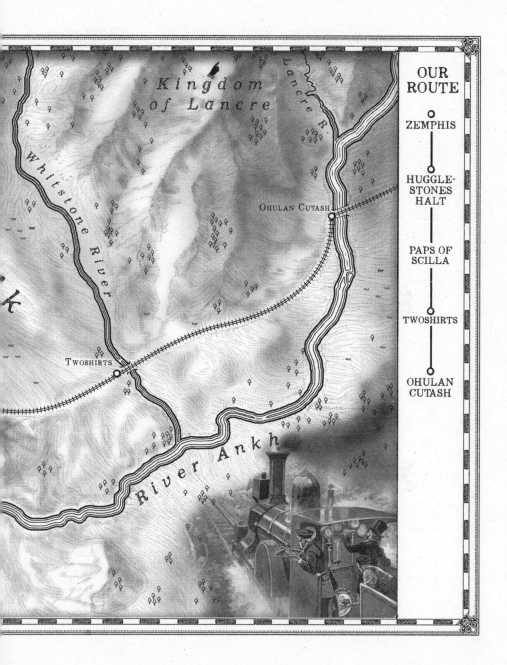

*Kingdom
of Lancre*

Lancre R.

Whitstone River

Ohulan Cutash

Twoshirts

River Ankh

**OUR
ROUTE**

ZEMPHIS

HUGGLE-
STONES
HALT

PAPS OF
SCILLA

TWOSHIRTS

OHULAN
CUTASH

6

—

The local service between Zemphis and Ohulan Cutash has now
been in operation for some time. However, at the time of writing
work is still continuing on the infrastructure of the track onward
from Ohulan Cutash to Bonk, to bring it to the necessary standard for
commercial traffic. When the promised international express comes into
service on this route, be assured that your author will be among its first
passengers. The first train from Zemphis leaves early in the morning,
and is favoured by those serious mountaineers who aim to climb the eight
summits of the Paps of Scilla (earning themselves a Papist Medal), or even
attempt the icy peaks of the Ramtops, as well as by holidaymakers planning
a gentler walking tour among the foothills. Other travellers will include
people visiting family in Lancre and The Chalk and dwarfs making the
long pilgrimage to the home mines of Copperhead Mountain.

The danger of rock falls and ambush by brigands on this journey means
that there are two railway watchmen keeping lookout on the footplate of
the locomotive as we leave the station. About half an hour out of Zemphis
and just before the train starts the long climb to the mountains it stops

at Hugglestones Halt, which serves the renowned Hugglestones School just across the bleak, windswept moorland. It was the start of the school's Spring Prime vacation on my visit and fifty or so boys poured on to the platform from open-topped coaches. The senior boys had their baggage carried by diminutive first-formers, bent double with the weight. Porters transported several stretcher- and wheelchair-bound boys into the luggage van, followed by two small coffins draped with the school flag. I have myself met some adult survivors of Hugglestones, where the boys of wealthy and titled families are educated in life's more rigorous challenges on blood-soaked playing fields, and have some sympathy for what they endured, but cannot for the life of me understand why they subject their children to the same brutality.

Within minutes of leaving Hugglestones Halt we are in the foothills of the Paps. This range was created when a huge mountain fell apart leaving eight razor-sharp peaks. The views from the train are spectacular: trees appear to cling to the sheer rock-face and rushing white-water streams run through deep ravines. Further towards the high pass the mountains close in, the towering slopes above us shutting out the sun, and from time to time there is a sudden blackness as the train enters a natural tunnel with water dripping from the roof and running down the windows. Eventually the descent begins towards the welcome sight of the small town of Twoshirts. It is not more than a hundred miles, as the crow flies, from Zemphis to Twoshirts, but the journey takes a good four hours because of the steepness of the gradients and the fact that the track, by a wonder of engineering, traverses chasms and steep ravines in a series of zigzags.

NOTE: The dining car on this route provides refreshment after the local style as we travel; it includes a most appetizing soup made from mushrooms grown by goblins in the mountain caves. It bolsters the heart as much as the stomach during the precipitous journey. The chef provided me with the recipe but did say the goblins add a secret ingredient which makes their soup much more than just a warming and tasty meal.

RECIPE: Of the Gill of the Shaggy Ear add five. Of the slippery stalk in the rain, one. Of the blushing toadstool, the caps of many. Of the white pebble the garlic. Under the waterfall the drips of an hour. To finish sprinkle of the brackets the spore.

•TWOSHIRTS•

POPULATION: *65*
CLACKS TERMINAL: *at the post office.*
POST OFFICE: *Counter in souvenir shop.*
ACCOMMODATION: *The Jolly Macerator Inn.*
MARKET DAY: *Friday.*

Situated on the Whitstone River, a tributary of the Ankh, Twoshirts was, and still is, a staging post on the way from Lancre to The Chalk. Since the arrival of the railway it has become a centre for walkers keen to explore the green downlands of The Chalk and the wooded river valleys near by. Mrs Umbridge's souvenir shop sells guidebooks and maps, walking sticks and waterproof clothing in a range of unnatural shades to

the visitors, as well as small carved wooden items and postcards. There is a daily haulier's cart that will carry passengers the slow five-hour journey to the village of Arken at the base of the Downs. The track passes a well-known landmark in the form of a great white horse cut into the chalk of the hillside.

Brassica from the Sto Plains is brought into Twoshirts by barge and then preserved by crushing the already stale yellowing cabbage leaves in barrels of salted vinegar. This bucolic activity is celebrated in the name of the village's inn, The Jolly Macerator, and dotted around the walls are pictures of this process. Proudly displayed in a glass case is a fine pair of huge leather lace-up boots, which, according to the brass plaque on the front, were worn by Mister Jackson Muchworthy who, if the size is anything to go by, must have been a champion macerator indeed.

Leaving Twoshirts on the final stage of our journey we approach the lower reaches of the great Ramtop mountains which loom large on the horizon, their snow-capped peaks clearly visible. The countryside is hilly with wooded areas, and in the winter months many grazing animals have to be brought down from the extreme cold of the mountains to these sheltered plains. The town of Ohulan Cutash which serves the needs of this rural community nestles beneath the rimward slope of a steep hill. Situated on the Upper Ankh River it is the transit point for the main road to the Kingdom of Lancre and has a small quay from which barges travel downstream all the way to Ankh-Morpork.

OHULAN •CUTASH•

POPULATION: 672
CLACKS TERMINAL: *at the railway station.*
ACCOMMODATION: *The Fiddler's Riddle, Barrack Farm Camp Site.*
BANK: *Thrift Bank.*
MARKET DAYS: *Wednesday (fruit and veg), Saturday (general).*
Artisan Cheese Festival, Spune.

The bandbox-new railway station has a small bookshop where they sell guidebooks and maps of the region. There is a large market square and on market day one may meet mountain folk, including dwarfs who work the Ramtop mines, as well as shoppers from Lancre, and invariably one or two black-hatted missionaries pressing explanatory pamphlets into shoppers' hands and inviting

them to visit the mission tent to partake of a cup of weak tea and the word of Om. The dwarf-run workshop offering a broom repair service is a salutary reminder that the long tradition of witchcraft in this part of the Disc has by no means expired. Indeed it seems you can buy almost anything here: musical instruments, ably demonstrated by the stall holder, herbal medicines from a small dark tent, tools, silver jewellery, crockery, clothing, haberdashery and all manner of foodstuffs including some very fine cheese. I imagine that this town will benefit from the additional trade that the railway has brought. Already there are establishments which specialize in selling camping equipment and climbing gear.

Sadly not all the holidaymakers who embark on mountaineering adventures respect the landscape

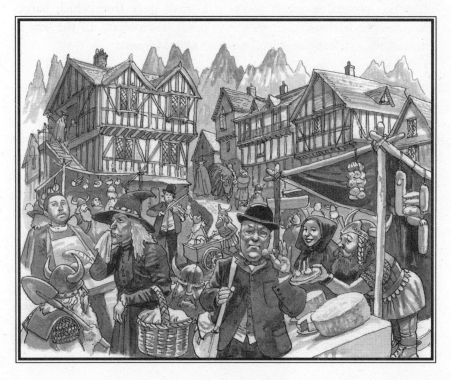

or take proper precautions; in the clear mountain air it all seems so safe and distances are deceptive. Following a series of unfortunate incidents it was decided something should be done. Apart from anything else reports had reached the Ankh-Morpork newspapers and it was not good for business.

The local lumberjacks and shepherds, who were often the ones to find the sad remains and who understand the treacherous nature of the weather, were the first to form an unofficial 'Rescue Off the Mountain Team', after a particularly distressing 'find'. Old habits die hard among mountain trolls and it seems that on this occasion a party of boy scouts had

pitched their camp and lit their fires on a particularly sensitive area of Big Alum who responded 'with extreme prejudice'. A local troll was quickly recruited to the rescue team to encourage mountain trolls to accept this invasion of city folk or at least to identify and map no-go areas. Dwarfs also joined the team in the wake of their retrieving a group of prospectors who had been sold a map of a goldmine while in Zemphis and had fallen into a disused shaft. They too produced a map of no-go areas, as well as helpfully marking spots where there was definitely no gold at all. A large donation from the AM&SPHR Co. topped up with money from local businesses has now funded a fully equipped mountain refuge and paid for the publication of a series of maps and guidebooks. The Ohulan Cutash Mountain Rescue Team now numbers more than twenty members, including goblins, who travel the hillsides with barrels of snail 'brandy'.

ACCOMMODATION AND REFRESHMENTS

TWOSHIRTS

THE JOLLY MACERATOR INN

Offers hospitality and good food to locals and travellers alike. A unique feature is the old macerating tub now on the terrace behind the inn, which has been converted to a communal bath.

OHULAN CUTASH

THE FIDDLER'S RIDDLE

A very good hostelry, that has been recently renovated with all modern facilities, and boasting ten large bedrooms. The dining is excellent and the bar friendly. Mr Skiller, the landlord, is also the town mayor and there is no doubt that he is extremely proud of his town and determined that its population will benefit from the coming of the railway.

BARRACK FARM CAMP SITE
This farmer is hoping to capitalize on the large numbers of visitors coming to Ohulan Cutash for the outdoor experience. At present there is little more on offer than a field which, as is fairly obvious even to a city-dweller, has only recently been cleared of livestock. Clean water and some hygienic arrangement is the least that travellers will expect.

Dear Reader,

It is time for me to leave the comfort, speed and safety of the railway, although there are still many journeys to be made. If like me you yearn to visit the lofty heights and magical realm of the Kingdom of Lancre, with its romantic tales of villages like Bad Ass, you may travel onwards on the mail coach up the long and steep road through the pine forests that cover this part of the Ramtops.

For those who wish to venture yet further afield to the dark forests and mountains of Uberwald I can recommend a little guide by the travel writer Boris Von Trappe called *My Adventures in Uberwald.*

I have enjoyed my voyages on the railway and I would like to thank all the people I have met along the way who have helped make my journey so pleasant and so interesting. I would especially like to thank Mr Lipwig for giving me this opportunity. I hope that my observations and notes will be of benefit to travellers for many years to come.

Thank you for purchasing this little book.

Georgina Bradshaw

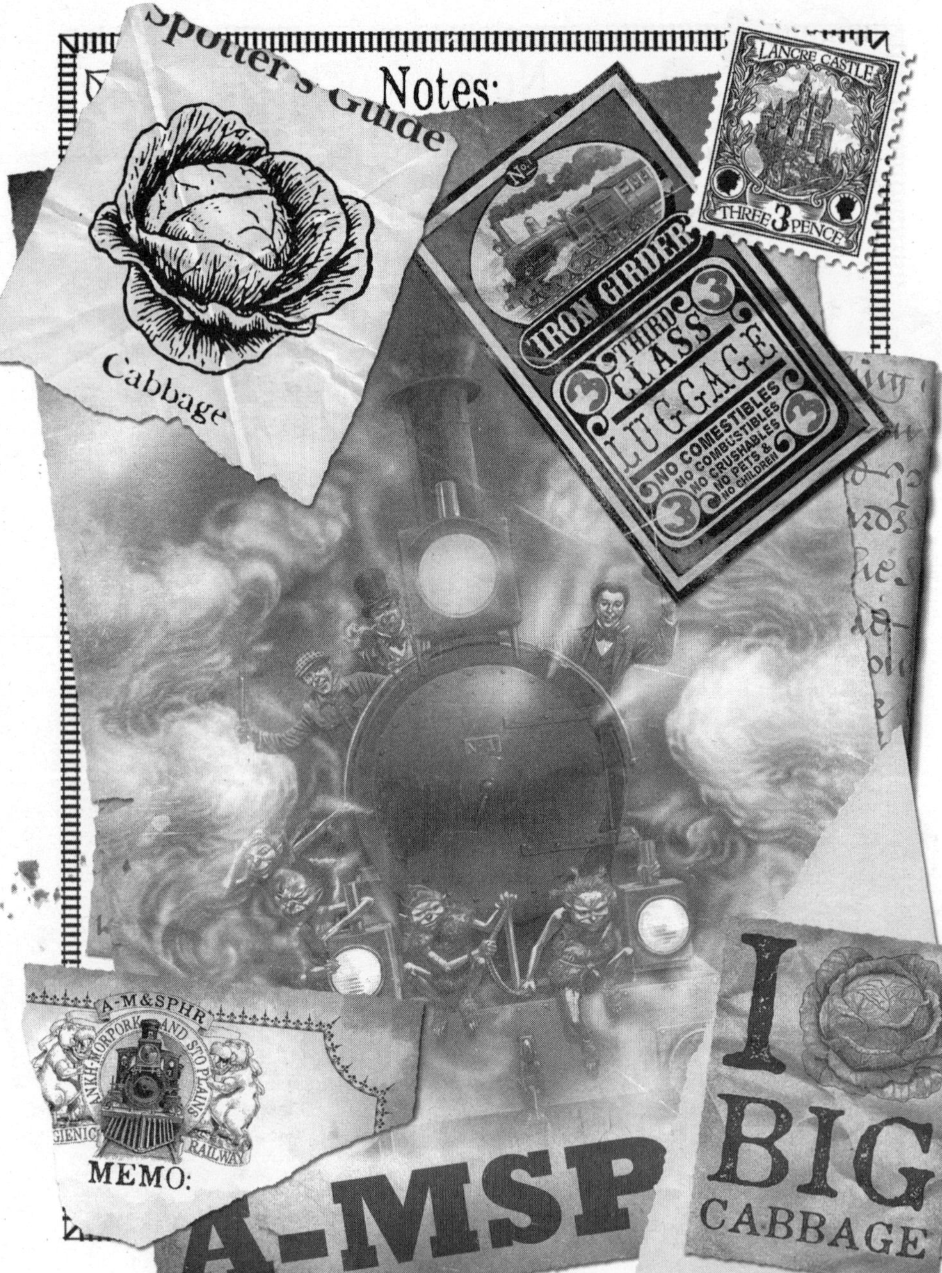

Spotter's Guide
Cabbage
Notes:
No. 1
IRON GIRDER
THIRD CLASS
LUGGAGE
NO COMESTIBLES
NO COMBUSTIBLES
NO CRUSHABLES
NO PETS &
NO CHILDREN
LANCRE CASTLE
THREE 3 PENCE
A-M&SPHR
ANKH-MORPORK AND STO PLAINS
GIENIC
RAILWAY
MEMO:
A-MSP
I
BIG
CABBAGE

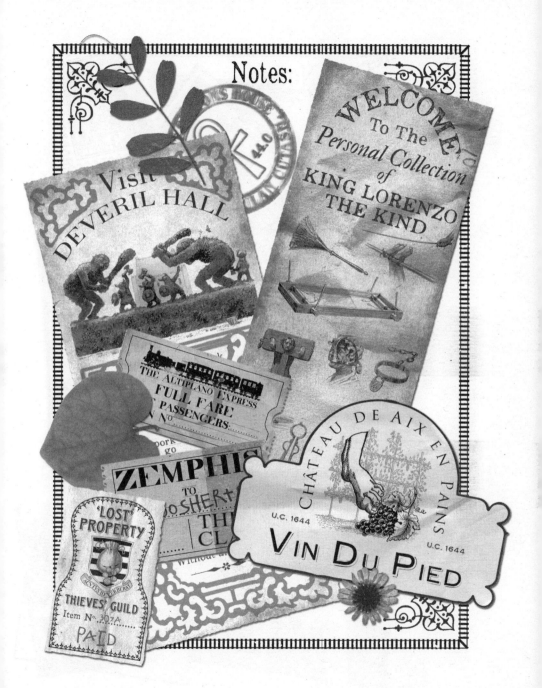

Notes:

Visit DEVERIL HALL

WELCOME
To The
Personal Collection
of
KING LORENZO
THE KIND

THE ALTIPLANO EXPRESS
FULL FARE
PASSENGERS
N°

ZEMPHIS
TO
SHER
TH
CL

'LOST'
PROPERTY
THIEVES' GUILD
Item N°. 307A
PAID

CHÂTEAU DE AIX EN PAINS
U.C. 1644
U.C. 1644
VIN DU PIED

Notes:

ANKH-MORPORK & STO PLAINS
RAILWAY
HYGIENIC
COMFORT & SAFETY
SPEED & SECURITY
TICKET №:
SEAT №:
ANKH-MORPORK - STO LAT
FIRST CLASS
SECOND CLASS
THIRD CLASS
RETAIN THIS PART